I0654127

LETTING GO

THE DEFIANT SISTERS- BOOK 1

DEFIANT SISTERS DUET
BOOK ONE

JACQUIE BIGGAR

WAVEFRONT PUBLISHING

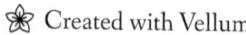

INTRODUCTION

A coming-of-age novel about the pain of misconceptions and learning from them.

When life gives you lemons...

Izzy

Mom is barely in the grave and the prodigal child is here to pick the bones clean.

I don't want her here. My sister's defection is a wound that won't heal and her return simply rubs at the scabs covering my heart.

I've managed just fine without her. She can go back to her fancy college and forget about us- that's what she does best anyway.

If only I didn't need her help. Or miss her so much.

Renee

The day my dad committed suicide I ran. I've been running ever since.

Going home is supposed to be the answer. Instead, it makes me question every thoughtless decision I've made.

My sister hates me. My little brother barely knows me. And Simon... is engaged.

None of it matters- or so I tell myself. I'm here to make amends and face a past haunted by regret.

As long as I can convince myself to stay.

Letting Go is a young adult romance dealing with tragedy, restitution, and love in all its aspects. The story relates to sensitive topics that may be triggering for some readers.

Secrets, Lies & Alibis

I've had the privilege of reading some of the previous books by this fantastic author, and this next installment is a wonderful addition to the series. Not only is this story a fast-paced action-adventure and romance, but it also emphasizes the strength of relationships, such as love and comradery between friends and family. It's a page-turning story and I give it five stars!!

— TAMMY- AMAZON REVIEWER

Perfectly Imperfect

More than just a romantic comedy, "Perfectly Imperfect" is the sprinkled donut in a big old box of regular glazed donuts of rom com fiction.

— REEDSY REVIEWER

The Sister Pact

This is a beautiful story about family, siblings, sisters, emotional healing, and true loves. Jacquie Biggar writes with perfection and infuses every story with warmth to touch a reader's heart. The Sister Pact is another perfect gem.

— MAE- AMAZON REVIEWER

For my critique group
Without your wise advice, this story wouldn't be the
same.
Thank you

PROLOGUE

RENÉE

I don't know why I agreed to come to this party. The noise level is just short of ear-splitting, the rooms are overcrowded, and everyone—except me, it seems—is either plastered or high. Simon is at the foosball table surrounded by his posse, who follows him *everywhere,* proving he's a star athlete off the field as well as on the pitch.

I'm glad he's having a good time, I am. It's just that today is my sister's birthday, sweet sixteen, and my graduation. I should be home celebrating with my family, especially since this is my senior year, and I probably won't be around for many traditional get-togethers for a while—not if I receive my scholarship to Berkeley, anyway.

A shiver of excitement scoots up my spine and I smile, catching the eye of a guy standing next to the bar. He raises a brow and starts across the sticky tile floor—the owners of this place are going to have a bird when they see the mess—obviously expecting to hook up. I flush and turn away, shoving through the heated bodies until I burst out the other end, like a gust of fresh air, and find myself on the patio. Though that seems like a tame word for this oversized terrace made up of stone and masonry. Big, heavy-looking clay pots filled with bamboo and cedar dot the surface, breaking the area into intimate nooks. Most have couples lolling on elegant wicker furniture, too caught up in each other to notice me edging by in the shadows. An infinity pool beckons, the water opaque and faintly sinister as it laps against the edge. Nervous giggles rise from the far side, and I squint, drawn by the familiarity of the sound.

Two silhouettes, reminding me of a statue I have in my bedroom, float near the stairs. The guy's arms are wrapped around the girl, holding her in place, and the glint of pale skin suggests an intimacy I'm not about to intrude on. I start to back away when the moon drifts from behind a cloud and limns the girl's head in an ethereal light highlighting flame-red hair I'd know anywhere.

"Elizabeth Mae Thomas, what do you think you're

doing?" My hands fly to my hips in outrage. My baby sister is... is naked in some random guy's arms. What the hell?

Izzy shrieks at the sound of my voice and hurries to cover budding breasts with her palms, a panicked expression overtaking the sensual haze of a moment ago.

Loverboy glides away and climbs the rungs, his scrawny buttocks shining wetly under the waning moon's glow. He has the decency to throw her a towel, before covering his arousal with another.

"Kyle, wait." Izzy shoots me an incensed glare, hair floating around her body like that of a merrow from our childhood storybooks.

"I better go." His voice is a mere breath of sound, but its ripples could be felt across the pool.

"No!" Izzy screeches then tempers her tone. "She can leave. Don't leave me here... like this." The last ends on a note of entreaty, and for a moment, I think the kid is going to stand up to me, but then he shrugs and backs toward the changing room.

"I'll see you tomorrow, okay?" he mumbles as an overhead light clicks on from his movement. It shines down, highlighting the scene—a stage from a play I never wanted to see.

I wait until the door closes behind him, then move

to help my sister, who's struggling to climb the steps while the wet towel drags her down.

"Give me your hand." I crouch near the edge, grateful for the stretchy skirt that clings to my thighs.

She looks up, mascara running, face pale, and... shoots a stream of water at me with her fist. "Bite me."

I gasp, caught off guard. Though, really, what did I expect? I'd just ruined her date, possibly her *first* date, though I couldn't be sorry. She's not ready for sex, she's still a kid, dammit.

Moisture dampens my blouse, sending goosebumps skittering up and down my arms as I stand back and wait for her to stumble onto the deck unaided. A burgundy swimsuit top lies near my feet and I grimace, imagining how it arrived there.

"Here." I hand it over between two pinched fingers, the material clammy from the pool.

"Thanks for nothing," she spits, defiantly dropping the towel with a sodden plop and gasping as the cold bra touches her skin. "You ruin everything. What are you doing here, anyway? Did you follow me?"

I can't help but see the disparity in our bodies, much like our temperaments. Whereas I'm easygoing, short and on the curvy side, Izzy is all legs, lean and spirited. Even though only eighteen months are separating us, sometimes it feels like a lifetime. She wears her heart on her sleeve and her passionate nature makes it hard to talk to her without it becoming a slinging match.

"Simon wanted to come." I shrug, knowing she won't believe me. "Why did you allow that boy those... liberties?" The word is a hard ball in my gullet. I'm worried. She tries too hard to fit in with the '*it*' crowd when half of them are not worth the air she breathes. Why can't she see that?

A harsh laugh covers tears she can't quite hide. "Is that what you call it? You're such a prude. No wonder Simon..."

I freeze, even my heart seems to still in my breast. "Simon's a good guy. I don't know what you're hinting at, and I don't want to hear it, either. This isn't about me, Izz. This is about you making a mistake you can never take back. Your innocence isn't something to give to the first boy to show you some attention. It's a precious gift to save for someone you love—don't rush it." I hold my hand out, hoping for a connection we haven't had in years, but there's no denying the sarcastic laughter sputtering from her throat.

"Is that what you did, sister dear?" She holds her belly as though it pains her. "Give your *gift* to perfect Simon, the boy you love? Well, I've got news for you, Renée, he likes to receive those *gifts* from half the cheerleading squad. I bet I could even..."

"Shut up," I cry, my hand closing in a fist. I've

never wanted to hit a person more than I do at this moment. In a far corner of my mind, I know she's lashing out because I caught her in a compromising position, but she's lying, Simon's not like that. He's sweet and kind and loyal. I would know if he was cheating. *I would know.* "Get dressed, I'm taking you home."

"Touched a nerve, did I?" she mocks. "I'll walk, thanks. You better go check up on your boyfriend. That's a big house—lots of bedrooms if you catch my drift." Her wink is triumphant. A statement of victory in a battle I came ill-equipped to fight.

"Five minutes," I tell her, fed up with the party, Simon, and my irritating sister. "I'll meet you out front."

"It must be tough keeping up that goody-two-shoes image you wear," she yells as I walk away, my spine so taut it might snap at any second.

How did we become enemies? As children, Izzy and I were inseparable. We laughed, played, bathed, and slept in the same bedroom, always together. Then our brother, Benjamin, was born and things changed. Ben seemed to get sick at the drop of a hat, which irritated our father and caused disharmony in the household. Izzy couldn't handle the tension and started to spend more and more time away from home, hanging with her weird school friends. We drew apart. But this, this bordered on hatred, and it hurts—a lot.

Anxious to escape my thoughts, I hurry into the sweltering house and search the undulating mob of partiers for my boyfriend. He isn't at the foosball table anymore, though a couple of his buddies still play.

Pushing through the throng, I sidle up to Marv and lightly touch his arm. "Did you see where Simon went?"

He lets his gaze roam my chest before slowly lifting to meet my narrowed eyes. "Maybe. What's in it for me?"

I shake my head and back away. "This is serious, you jerk. Where is he?"

"Don't be a dick," Jim snorts with an embarrassed laugh. "Ignore him, Renée, he's cranky because he's losing. Simon's at the bar grabbing drinks. He should be back soon if you want to wait."

"Thanks, but I think I'll give him a hand. Good luck with the game." I can't resist the parting shot as I turn to weave around the group betting on the match's outcome. Simon is at the counter with his back to me, mahogany hair glinting under the dim overhead lighting. Relieved, I hurry to intercept him before we get separated in the mob—did Peterson invite the whole school?—shoving me this way and that, a tide I can't wade through. But then, I stop in my tracks for the second time tonight as the room drops away revealing *my* boyfriend in the arms of another girl. I blink, refusing to accept what my eyes are telling me.

She's pretty if you like busty blondes with pink highlights in their hair and sleazy dresses about two sizes too small. Apparently, Simon does, because his hands are planted on the curves of her ass and her hands are discovering braille on his pecs—and lower. Stomach-churning, I let the flowing crowd carry me away.

If only I'd known that wasn't the worst thing I'd see that night.

CHAPTER ONE

RENÉE

T*wo years later*

The town looks the same as when I left for college. The *Welcome to Smuggler's Cove, pop. 7562,* sign bows with the weight of the old town's worries on its aged wooden frame. God, I'm glad I escaped.

My second-hand SUV chugs up the hill and over the bridge. Chinook, the river named after the salmon who travel hundreds of miles to spawn in its muddy brown water, gurgles over the rocks far below. Giant rubber tubes in a rainbow of colors filled with laughing teens dot the surface. I'd joined them many times to get away from the oppression at home.

Home.

It's been nearly two years since I left, and would've

been longer if I had my choice. Hard on the heels of guilt come the ever-ready tears. Fact is, while I soaked up the west coast sunshine and campus life, my little sister had taken over the reins of the house, getting my brother to school, paying the bills, and caring for Mom.

Someone honks their horn, an angry *watch it* sound. Startled, I jerk the wheel and almost cream the rail. Nervous laughter pushes through clenched teeth. Wonder what Miss Perfect would say to that? Mom never understood the jealousy that reared its ugly head around Izzy. Hell, I didn't get it myself. It just is.

The restaurant my friends and I haunted throughout high school comes up on the right. Why hadn't I noticed how old and tired it looked? The door opens and a group of four exits into the parking area.

Simon.

My heart drops to my toes. He glances away from the woman laughing up at his handsome face and our eyes meet. Time slows. Everything we'd done together, been together, lost together plays out in my mind like a tragic Shakespearean play. *God, why now?* I'd hoped to sneak into town, do my duty, and leave with no one the wiser.

He steps away from his date—a blonde like me—and lifts his hand as though to wave me down. The others turn to see what's going on and I—being the scaredy-cat my sister always accused me of—punch the gas pedal and grimace as my vehicle belches out a plume of dark gray smoke before obeying my command.

Damn. What else could go wrong?

And isn't that just the stupidest question ever?

The turn for our street comes up too fast. I drive by, then have to circle the block. Avoiding the situation isn't going to make it go away. Mom is still...

Our house looks just the same; a two-bedroom craftsman Daddy converted into four by finishing the basement for his girls. That's what he'd called Izzy and me, his beautiful baby girls. We'd grown up poor, but it never felt that way. Our parents always made sure we had new outfits for school, birthday parties all the neighborhood kids clamored to attend, and Christmases where we could hardly find the floor for all the gifts. We were spoiled but in a good way. We understood the value of money and knew we had to take care of our stuff or face severe punishment—usually, a week of doing dishes by ourselves, washing and drying. Dad worked long hours at the tire shop and Mom took in mending and baking for the local market. My job was to babysit my brother and sister and keep them out of Dad's hair until he had a chance to relax after work, which meant chugging back a beer or three.

I can't make myself pull into the driveway, it feels too much like getting sucked into a void, so I parallel park in front of the house and shut down the engine. Over the click of the cooling motor, I hear the birds chattering in our towering Lodgepole Pine tree that shades most of the yard and part of the road. We used to take turns seeing how high we could climb as kids, even though Mom said if we broke our necks we were on our own. Izzy, the little tomboy, had scurried from branch to branch like there were suction cups attached to her feet and hands. Ben was only five or six maybe and scared of heights. I could get him to hang onto the bottom branches, but that was as far as he would go. But, his smile. It made the fact I was stuck on the ground watching him worthwhile.

We'd tried to talk Mom into moving after Dad... but she wouldn't hear of it. She said this house held the key to every happy memory she could recall; from arriving as a young, naïve bride, to pregnancy, babies, and holidays. She refused to throw it all away because of our father's last, selfish act. And that was that. We all pretended the backyard didn't exist and carried on as though our lives were normal when they were anything but.

The gate creaks open with a lisp, the hinges old and rusty and barely holding onto the whitewashed fence. Grass grows better between the sidewalk blocks than in the rest of the yard, littered with pine needles and the cones Mom used to send us out to collect for craft night. My heel catches in one of the hairline cracks in the cement and I nearly fall on my face. It's the final straw; I turn to leave, tomorrow is another day, but the door opens and I stop in my tracks.

Izzy.

She looks older. A nervous laugh bubbles. I wasn't expecting it to be this hard. "Hi." That's me, Miss Eloquent.

"What are you doing here?" She leans a slim shoulder against the door frame, her red hair glinting in the sun, her gaze flat and hooded. The dark circles underneath her green eyes tug on my heartstrings. Well, that and the sorrow engulfing me the moment she opened the door. There's no more denying it— Mom is gone.

I ignore her antagonism and hurry forward, dropping my overnight bag at our feet—so different, me in my heels, her barefoot—and draw her resisting body into my arms. I close my eyes, the better to breathe in the essence of my baby sister. Every bit as strong and lean as I remember, her arms are stiff and unyielding at her sides. Heaven forbid she'd give in to a moment of sentimental emotion.

Forgiveness isn't big on the Thomas's list of strong points.

Reluctant, I let her go and take a step back to assess how she's holding up. Not good, if the too-pale skin and deep lines across her forehead are anything to go by. Well, I'm here now. It's past time I take on some of the family responsibilities.

"Where's Ben?" I ask, glancing over her shoulder into the dim hallway beyond. "Is he...?" What could I say? Doing okay? Upset? Sad? Mad? No doubt, all of those and more. Benjamin was closest to Mom, her baby. It wouldn't be easy for him to accept her death. An ugly shiver sweeps down my back.

"He's in his room. He doesn't come out. I can't get thr... what does it matter?" Izzy snarls, tossing her head. "You didn't care before. You can't just show up, especially now, and expect everything to be how it was when we were kids. There's no going back." She straightens and heads inside, trying to slam the door in my face.

Good to know her temper is the same, anyway. I stop the door with my palm, wincing as the pressure explodes up my arm. Much as I want to leave, the time for running is over.

I'm home.

CHAPTER TWO

IZZY

The shock of finding Renée on the doorstep is fading, taken over by the sheer hypocrisy of her arrival. Why now? It's a little late if she wants to make amends. Not a word for two stinking years and she shows up thinking I'm going to be grateful she's here?

Not in this lifetime.

The warm sincerity of her embrace, though... it tries to weaken the resentment I've fostered since she walked out on her family, leaving me to pick up the pieces.

"I don't want you here," I snarl, unable to hide my bitterness. I'd rather act as though I don't care.

Renée eyes me warily, rubbing a reddened palm. I

feel a childish delight to have caused her even a minuscule amount of the pain she's caused me.

"I'm aware," she says calmly, bending to pick up a bulging overnight bag. "But I'm here now, so let's make the best of it—for Mom."

Red hot rage rises from the pit of my stomach to spit and steam from my ears. "*Do. Not.* Use Mom against me. You lost that right a long time ago."

Months of caregiving flicker behind my eyes. My father's suicide did something to Mom. She shouldered the blame and wore it like a hairshirt, ripping the blinders away from their relationship to show the fractures in the foundation. She shut down. Stopped eating, washing, and caring. It was left to me to get Benjamin off to school, clothes washed, and a semblance of normalcy when everything was insane.

"You should have called." Renée's empathetic gaze gets on my last nerve.

I whirl away before I plant my fist in her face. "Your room is the way you left it. You can stay the weekend, then I want you to leave. Ben doesn't need to get his hopes up." *And neither do I.*

Striding into the kitchen, I clench my hands over the lip of the sink and hang my head. The stack of unpaid bills mocks my independence, but it's the manila folder that strikes fear in my heart.

"What did you mean by that?"

Startled, I jerk around, careful to place my body in front of the envelopes. "Nothing. You can go now. I have things to do. Unless you want to mow the backyard?" I don't know why I said that. The shocked horror on my sister's face should have filled me with triumph but it only leaves me with the urge to cry.

"Renée..." I make an aborted attempt at an apology, but she waves it away.

"I'm going to grab us something to eat. It was a long drive and I'm starved. I'll be back soon." And with that she was gone, the lone overnight bag sitting on the floor the only sign she'd been here, and it wasn't a figment of my imagination.

The front door closes, and I sink to the floor, the dust and crumbs barely making an impression on the turmoil in my head.

How did she know to come now? Someone (not me) tracked her down with news of Mom's death. I flat-out refused. If she'd stayed instead of running away, she would have known what was going on. How Mom started taking pills and sleeping all day. How she quit talking—even to Ben, who didn't understand why—and spent hours staring at the wall, waiting to die, though I didn't realize it then.

I rest my head on bent, bony knees—I'd lost so much weight I barely recognized myself anymore—and close my eyes, just for a minute. I haven't slept properly in too long, that's why I gave in to Renée. It has nothing to do with how very lonely I am. Or how frightened I am that Benjamin will be taken away and I'll never see him again.

Then, it would be just me.

All alone.

Sighing, I get up like an old woman, grasping the counter for balance, then totter down the grimy hall to my little brother's bedroom. My knock goes unanswered, and I debate leaving him to his privacy, but dammit, he's twelve, not eighteen. He should be running and playing and spending time with friends. It's bad enough he hasn't been to school since Mom died, I can't keep letting him fade away like this. Like Mom did.

Opening the door, I poke my head in. He's lying on his back, feet crossed and arms straight out from his sides. He slowly turns his head to glance at me then goes back to his inspection of our popcorn ceiling.

"Hey, Bud, guess who's here?"

He shrugs disinterestedly. "If it's that lady from the school, I don't want to see her."

Mrs. Bains means well, but she thinks going back to class is the answer to moving on after the deaths of your parents. I could tell her she's misinformed but I'm already walking a tightrope with the school, I don't need to stir shit up.

I stroll into Ben's room and trail my fingertips over his dusty dresser. There's always something to clean. I don't know how Mom kept up to it when we were kids. I've gained new respect. Too bad it came too late to count for much.

I bypass the framed portrait—a snapshot of happier days—and move on to his collection of superheroes. He has the toy figurines lined along the bottom of the beveled mirror as though they're waiting for a calamity before rushing off to save the world. Except, they forgot to show up when we needed them the most.

I take the two steps to the narrow, single bed and gingerly sit on the edge. Who knows when these sheets were last changed, they smell as musty as the rest of the house.

Ben watches me with amber eyes that see too much. I brush the hair from his forehead. It needs cut, but I barely have money for milk never mind a barber.

"Renée showed up a while ago," I blurt, relieved to have someone to tell.

His expression undergoes a transformation, and he sits up, his gaze wide. "Really? Where is she?"

"Gone to get dinner, should be back soon." I try to stifle my jealousy, but it leaks through, anyway. "I guess I should have led with that if it gets you out of this bed."

He has the sense to look sheepish. "It's been a long time. I missed her, is all."

I ruffle his curly mop. "I know. Hurry up and have a shower. You want to look good when she gets back, don't ya?"

He starts to scramble off the thin mattress but stops long enough to give me a too-quick hug. "Maybe, she'll stay this time," he whispers.

I don't have the heart to tell him otherwise.

"Maybe," I whisper back, my throat tight. "We'll see."

CHAPTER THREE

SIMON

Lacey knows something is wrong, but I can't bring myself to tell her about Renée—not yet. Old feelings I'd thought dead and buried roil in my chest, demanding to be set free. I'd waved like a fool when she'd driven by as though two years and a thousand recriminations didn't lay between us. Why did she have to come home now?

Jim and Marv say something and give me a nudge but it's all white noise. I can't seem to focus on anything other than the taillights disappearing down the road. Is she here to stay? Her family was destroyed after her father killed himself. I see Izzy occasionally; she's a barista over at The Voltage, but we carefully avoid any mention of Renée. It's too hard to think of her without the accompanying anger and regret. I could have, should have, been more understanding of what she was going through, but in all honesty, she checked out on our relationship long before it imploded.

"So you agree, then?" Jim demanded, finally breaking through the fog in my head.

"What are you yammering about? I swear you two are worse than a couple of old men." I grin and wrap an arm around Marv's neck to give him a nuggy.

"Ow!" He slips out of my hold and rubs at the pink spot on his forehead. "I was just sayin' this wedding needs a big moment, okay?"

"I think it's big enough already unless you're buying," I retort.

"Really?" Lacey looks at me with hurt blue eyes.

Aw, shit. I'm going to kill Marv later.

I reach for her hand and pull her into my arms. "We'll talk about this in private. These idiots are troublemakers." I send them a *watch-it* glare, then bend to kiss her pouting lips, and try not to compare them to another bow-shaped mouth I can't seem to forget.

"C'mon, bro, we're trying to help," Jim the Peacekeeper says.

"Speak for yourself," Marv declares. "He's got the girl, the job, the car... it doesn't hurt him to fork out the cash."

The barely covered bitterness doesn't go unnoticed. I meet my friend's gaze and acknowledge the jealousy he carries like a dirty blanket. Marv's a great guy with a dark cloud over his head. Whereas anything I tackle seems to work out—with one notable exception —it all goes to crap for Marv. Still, if we're buddies the way he keeps swearing we are, we should have each other's back—thick or thin and all that crap.

"I work for that money, same as you," I reply, unwilling to get into it with him in the middle of the parking lot. I've held two jobs since I was a punk-nosed kid. Money was tight at home and I like nice things. In those earlier years, it meant fancy hightops and designer jeans. Later, it paid my way into medical tech training and got me the car of my dreams—a 1967 Plymouth Barracuda fastback coupe—in forest green. There's no way I'm going to apologize for having ambition. Maybe Marv could use a dose of it himself.

"Are we still on for the fair next week?" Jim asks, shaking his head and rolling his eyes from over Marv's shoulder.

"If I'm not on shift." Lacey's shoulders turn to stone under my arm and I inwardly wince.

"You promised to take me to the dance." She stares up at me as though I took her puppy. "I bought a new dress and everything." The last comes out in that ear-piercing whine she's adopted whenever things aren't going her way. I remember thinking it was kind of cute, but now it just seems childish—which doesn't bode well for the next twenty-five years of matrimonial bliss I'd been looking forward to.

"Lace, you know I'm a low man on the totem pole with the EMS service. If they need me, I can't say no. But," I hasten to add as her blue-sky eyes turn stormy. "I mentioned it to the captain and he took me off the roster, so we should be on for Saturday night barring any catastrophes. Jim, that means you." I look over and chuckle as his ears turn red.

"How was I supposed to know I'd have a panic attack riding the Tilt-A-Whirl?"

"Seriously? That's a kiddie ride." Lacey gives Jim a disparaging glance. She's never liked my buddies and enjoys taking them down a peg or two whenever the opportunity arises. We almost came to blows when I informed her they would be my best men, but I stuck to my guns. Jim, Marv, and I have been like brothers my whole life, they aren't going anywhere.

"We'd better get going," I hurry to say before Jim tells my bride-to-be what he really thinks. "I have to be at the station soon."

"Keep the wheels on the road, man." Jim wraps his hand around my inner arm and gives it a rough shake. "You and that damn hero complex of yours."

I smile but wonder if that's what they truly believe.

It's not a hero complex to want to help those in need, is it? If my friends can't understand my drive to become a paramedic, then they don't know me at all.

Tabling those morose thoughts for a quieter moment, I give the guys a last wave and lead Lacey to my car and open the passenger door to let her in. She makes slithering onto the leather seat an erotic dance with her tight dress and long, long legs. Another time I would have taken her up on the suggestive offer, but even if I wasn't heading to work, I would have had to pass. Seeing Renée had brought up a lot of old feelings I need to process before I can give Lace the commitment she deserves.

I gently close her door and round the back of the 'Cuda to climb behind the driver's wheel. The car starts with a low-throated rumble that sends a predictable thrill coursing up my spine.

"Seatbelt, sweetheart," I remind her as I click mine into place and put the shifter into gear.

She turns in her seat and stares at me. "Do you love me, Simon?"

I frown. "We're getting married, aren't we?"

"That's not an answer."

No, it wasn't. But for the life of me, I can't utter the reassurances she wants to hear, either. I'm very much afraid Renée's reappearance will once again change my life.

CHAPTER FOUR

RENÉE

In town, barely an hour and I'm already contemplating escape routes—not a great way to start my road to redemption. I'd forgotten how good my sister is at slinging barbs and rub my chest, sure they have embedded themselves into my damaged soul. I deserve every harsh gibe she levered my way, but it doesn't make them any easier to bear.

It takes a few tries to jab the key into the ignition with tears dripping off my chin and plopping into my lap. It would be easier for everyone if I leave, just drive over the Chinook bridge and keep on going.

I put the SUV into gear and carefully pull onto the street, using the bottom of my shirt to wipe my face. This is a mistake. Izzy doesn't want me here. I should return to Berkeley, bury myself in work and books, and forget I ever thought of getting my family back.

Too bad guilt won't let me carry through on that decision.

Careful to avoid the Cedar Café and any chance meetings with Simon and his friends, I stick to the outer fringes of town, surprised by how much it's changed. Box stores have claimed acres of real estate along the main road leading in and out of town and seem to be thriving, going by the packed parking lots. New subdivisions, cropped up around them, are filled with cookie-cutter houses my dad would have hated on principle. He always maintained a happy home had to have character, something to distinguish it from its neighbor. Not a problem with our house. It looked like it was built from a hodge podge of leftover pieces; Victorian gables on the front porch, colonial columns holding up the second floor, and a wraparound deck straight out of *Country Homes*.

But it was ours.

Which made it even more heartbreakingly sad we'd lost not one but both of our parents within its walls. Or fence line.

Even though it's bright and sunny outside, I turn the heater on high and shiver behind the wheel as the funeral home grows like a big black monolith in my front windshield. Made from Carmanah marble quar-

ried nearby, it refracts light as though the spirits themselves seek to escape. In a little over a week, we will be
saying our last goodbyes to our mother in its tasteful
chapel. It hurts just thinking about it. We hadn't
always seen eye-to-eye, but I never doubted her love.
Even when others judged me as lacking.

Poor Momma. She spent her life trying to do the
best she could for us and look where it got her—laid out
on a cold slab in the morgue. I couldn't contemplate the
whys of it or it would drive me crazy. I wanted to lay
the blame at Daddy's feet, but I was the catalyst. If I'd
stayed, she'd still be here—end of the story. And that's
something I have to live with for the rest of my life.

A banner fluttering in the wind catches my attention and I signal, crossing the lane to turn once there is
a lull in oncoming traffic. A fair is coming to town. I'd
forgotten the summer jamborees when Main Street
takes on the look of a carnival complete with a Ferris
wheel covered in multi-colored lights, bumper cars, a
kiddie's roller coaster ride, haunted houses, games of
chance, and of course, food trucks with sugar-coated
elephant ears, sticky, rainbow-hued cotton candy, giant
corn dogs and hamburgers loaded with fried onions.
Izzy and I used to beg, borrow, and plead until we were
allowed to go; first with our parents tagging along, then
later with school friends and *boys*. My first kiss
happened on top of the Ferris wheel. Fourteen and

madly in love with Travis Donaldson, or so I thought until he dumped me a day later for Lottie Forbes and her boobs. Izzy knew how mortified I was and put out a rumor that Travis had STDs. I don't think we even knew what they were back then, but it worked; Travis became the ninth-grade laughingstock and ended up moving to another school. I never told my sister, but she turned my humiliation into a victory.

Mind on the past, I almost miss the elderly woman who popped out from between two parked cars and jaywalked directly in front of my vehicle. Heart in my throat, I stomp on the horn and my brakes at the same time, skidding to a stop as her gray head disappears from view.

I just hit a senior citizen.

Afraid of what I'll find, I shove my door open and slide from the cab, vaguely aware traffic had slowed, and pedestrians were hurrying to the poor woman's aid.

"I'm so, so sorry." I push through the growing crowd and drop to my knees next to the fallen lady. "Mrs. O'Brian?"

Watery blue eyes blink up at me from the wizened face of my ex's grandmother, her expression confused. "What... happened?"

I grasp her hand, petrified I'd injured her in some way. "I think I may have hit you with my car. Does anything hurt? Your head?" I glance around, noting the phones pointing our way. "Did someone call 911? Please, give her room to get some air."

"Ambulance is on the way," a helpful motorist said, waving his cell phone in the air. And sure enough, the mournful wail could be heard in the distance.

"Help is coming, Mrs. O'Brian, hold on." I squeeze her fingers and try a reassuring smile that wobbles alarmingly. I've never been in a car accident before, though this is more like a hit and run even if I didn't run, and oh my gosh am I going to get arrested for running over my ex-boyfriend's grandmother?

"I'm a doctor. Let me have a look." A burly man with steel-gray hair and a jacquard sweater cut through the motley of bystanders to squat on the other side of the increasingly fidgety patient. "Well, Katherine, what have you done now?" And just when my hackles rise at his disparaging comment, he runs gentle hands up and down her ribs, neck, and hips. "There are better ways to cross the street, young lady."

His voice seems to calm Mrs. O'Brian. She gives him a coquettish look from under damp eyelashes. "Reginald, were we supposed to meet here?"

He chuckles and puts an arm under frail shoulders to help her to a sitting position. The wail of the sirens is louder now, and the crowd starts to draw back, some waving to get the EMT's attention. "Next time, use the crosswalk, will you?"

She frowned. "I thought I did."

I stand as the medics arrive. The driver hops out and nods to the doctor before shifting to stabilize the victim. She argues, insisting she's on a date with the doctor and will leave when she's ready. I'm not sure if her confusion comes from the accident or is something else, but my heart aches for her, nonetheless.

The second EMT hurries through the crowd hauling medical bags in his muscular arms. The dark blue uniform molds to strong thighs and a brawny chest. Curiosity stirs and I lift my gaze and freeze, shock coursing through my veins.

Simon.

He drops to his knees and cradles his grandmother's hand, brows drawn and mouth hard. "Grams, what happened?"

She lifts her free hand to pat his cheek as I've seen her do many times in the past. "It's nothing, sweetheart. I was crossing the street and the nice girl ran me down, that's all. Everyone is making such a fuss. Take me home, Simon, will you?" She tries to sit up again, and Simon urges her to rest even as his gaze searches the crowd around my vehicle, his icy glare burning as it falls on my face.

Time stands still. The crowd fades away until

there's only the two of us. I have the insane urge to run into his arms, let him sweep me off my feet, and rain kisses on my lips like he's done so many times in the past. His eyes flare as though he knows what I'm thinking but then his partner says something and the scene fragments.

They wheel her away on a stretcher, the doctor following, and I turn to go back to my vehicle but freeze at the sight of two police officers waiting near the open driver's door.

"We need a word with you, Miss."

CHAPTER FIVE

SIMON

Even as I check my grandmother's vitals and assess her for injuries, my mind is spinning. Is it true? Did Renée just run her over? Did she do it on purpose? Of course not. I don't know where that thought even came from. Renée is many things, but vindictive isn't one of them. Why do our families clash this way? It ruined our relationship and broke my heart once before, I refuse to let her get under my skin again.

"What hurts, Grandma?" I gently clip on a neck brace to protect her spine until x-rays can confirm she's okay.

"My pride," she retorts. "I feel like an old fool."

"Aah, Katherine, you're ageless." Dr. Dunsmuir

tips an imaginary hat and teases a tired chuckle from her slightly blue lips.

I add an oxygen tube to her nose and nod for my partner to move out. "We're going to take a ride to the hospital, Grandma. If you're good, Dobbs here might even turn on the lights and sirens for you."

As predicted, she swats my arm and frowns. "I'm not dying yet, young Simon. Just get me home in time for my soap opera and you'll remain my favorite grandson."

I chuckle as we carefully lift her feather-light body onto the stretcher and buckle her in. "Nice try, but I'm you're only grandson."

"Well then, all the more reason to do as I ask, isn't it?" she retorts with some of her old verve before lying back and closing her blue-veined eyelids.

Dobbs signals up and we both stand back and let the hydraulics lift the bed in preparation for transport. I key the mic and update our ETA, gather the medic bag, and smile at Dr. Dunsmuir. "I imagine you're following us in?"

He nods and squeezes Grandma's hand. "I hear the hospital puts out a good lunch. She's not reneging on our date that easily."

The crowd of curious onlookers steps away as we begin the trek to the waiting ambulance. I notice their attention shifting to something over my shoulder and I glance back, expecting to see Renée driving away in that rattletrap she calls a vehicle. Instead, I catch a glimpse of flashing red and blue lights. My feet stop moving and the grip on the stretcher slips until I let go as Dobbs continues blithely on his way. Two officers are talking to Renée and judging by their posture, it's not going well.

Without thinking, I take a step in their direction, protective feelings jumping to the fore. Renée notices and her eyes widen. She shakes her head once, hard, and turns away, effectively shutting me out. I don't know why I'm surprised, it's what she does best.

Sighing, I hurry to catch up to Dobbs just as he reaches the back of the ambulance. He lets his gaze stray to Renée before raising a brow in my direction.

"Problem?"

I'm not sure if he's talking about the cops or the blonde, but I can guess. "Nope, it's all good." I grab the stretcher behind Grandma's head, ready to direct it into the ambulance when the lift elevates it into place. "Ready, Grandma?"

She jerks and raises her hand in a weak wave. "Let's get this over with. I hate causing a stir. I just want to go home."

I'm afraid she might be disappointed. At seventy-five, her bones are not as strong as they used to be. The hospital will do a barrage of tests to check for underlying injuries before Grams gets her wish. I feel sorry for the staff, she can be a handful.

"I know, but you need to let the doctors do their job. I'll call Mom, she can meet us there."

"Do *not* call your mother. You know how she worries over everything. I'm a stupid old woman who should have been watching where she was going. I don't need to have a keeper to tell me that."

Dobbs grins at my discomfiture. "I like your grandmother," he says, reaching for a gray hospital blanket to wrap around her shivering form.

Reaction is kicking in. As soon as we get underway, I'll check her vitals again to make sure she's stable. The stretcher bumps gently into place and I hop in after and begin setting up my workstation while Dobbs closes the doors, then goes around front to the driver's seat.

"Won't be long now. Hang on, okay?" I pat her hand and, noting the chilly skin, tuck both of them under the blanket.

"I did a dumb thing, didn't I?" she whispers, her eyes teary. "They're going to lock me away for certain now."

Lock her away? I knew my parents had looked into senior living accommodations for when Grandma couldn't manage on her own, but surely not if she isn't ready to make the move.

"Let's not jump to conclusions before we learn what the doctor has to say. I'm sure Mom and Dad only want what's best for you."

"Or for them," she mutters under her breath.

I pretend not to hear and instead, pull out the stethoscope and place it on her breastbone. The slightly raised heartbeat is to be expected considering our conversation, but the flush on her cheeks contrasting with the paleness of her skin worries me.

"What's our ETA?" I ask Dobbs.

He glances over his shoulder, then returns to the road ahead. "Ten minutes, give or take. Need a rush put on it?"

I smile reassuringly at Grandma. "You promised the lady some lights and sirens, remember?" The best I could do to relay my concern without frightening the patient.

Dobbs chuckles. "Well, can't disappoint the guest of honor, can we?" He flips a switch and the undulating screech of the siren put an end to our exchange.

I grasp Grandma's hand under the covers, try to get comfortable on the narrow bench running along the wall of the van, and wonder if this will send Renée running again.

CHAPTER SIX

IZZY

The scents and sounds of the busy coffee shop wrap around me, easing the stress I've been carrying ever since my sister showed up on our doorstep. From French Press to Espresso, cappuccino to macchiato, The Voltage serves it all and is a hit with the millennials.

"An Americano and a Cortado." A woman steps up to the counter and rummages in an oversized leather handbag, Gucci sunglasses pushed carelessly on top of shoulder-length cornsilk hair.

"Coming right up." I hand the order over to Jay, my boss, the best barista in the state, and ring up the tab. She finally locates her wallet in that suitcase she calls a purse and taps a platinum Mastercard—of course—over the POS machine, then waits impatiently for her receipt. Fingers with pink-tipped nails delicately pick up the assigned number card and without once meeting my gaze, she leaves the lineup streaming out the door and takes a two-seater at the window.

Shrugging off the encounter, I breeze through the next ten customers, then move to give Jay a hand at the coffee station.

"Steady morning," he says, pulling the steam wand and holding a chilled metal pitcher in place as microfoam with the texture of shiny wet paint and tiny, uniform bubbles fill the container. Next, he carefully pours the mixture over fragrant espresso nestled into a light blue bone china cup, creating a delicate Rosetta design.

"Latte for thirty-one," he calls out, placing the cup and saucer on the glass shelving that separates the work area from the public space. A guy in chinos and a plaid shirt with a tote hanging over one shoulder steps up and takes the cup with a smile highlighting cute twin dimples. I bestow an answering quirk on my lips, because why not, and wipe down the workstation with a bleach-scented, snow-white cleaning rag.

"Another happy customer." I nudge Jay's tattooed hand out of my way and squeal at the warm milk he drizzles over my fingers. "Hey! Watch it, Mister."

He chuckles and leans close to whisper in my ear. "Lucky for you we're in public or I'd lick them clean."

A shiver coasts over my spine and lodges in my stomach, causing butterflies to stir. Whether it's his words or the warmth of his breath against my sensitive neck, I'm not sure, but the guy is seriously hot—and my boyfriend of six months. Not that we're announcing our relationship to anyone. My choice, not his. Jay is great, but I'm not ready to commit to anything serious. KISS. Keep it simple stupid is my motto. That way no one—meaning me—gets hurt.

"What time are you coming over tonight?" He cocks a hip against the stainless-steel counter and crosses one foot over the other, a dark brow raised enquiringly.

I realize I'm wringing the cloth to death and set it down before he picks up on my anxiety and asks questions I can't answer. "My sister is in town—raincheck?"

His eyes see too much and it's all I can do to retain my nonchalant façade. He's been a rock since Mom died, I don't want to lay my complex feelings about Renée at his feet. I don't even understand them myself.

He tips my chin with gentle fingers that bring ready tears I try to blink away, cursing under my breath. "I'm here if you need me. You can talk to me, you know that, right?"

Hiccupping out a watery chuckle, I swipe wet

cheeks with trembling fingers. "Be careful. If I start, I may never stop."

Concern turns his eyes espresso dark. He straightens and takes a step toward me just as the bell over the door announces a new customer. Impatience flashes before he reins it in and squeezes my arm reassuringly. "Let's take this up later, call me after work."

The request couched as a demand should have gotten my ire up—I don't like being told what to do—but it's coming from a place of caring, and I know that, so I simply nod and turn to greet the next coffee buff to wander into our shop. The man is tall, his profile as he scans the occupants of the café's twelve bistro tables, chiseled with sharp cheekbones and a chin carved from the granite that encapsulates so much of the area.

My biggest mistake.

"Kyle, I thought you were in New York?" I stutter out a greeting, far from the normal cool chick I work so hard to portray.

He turns crystalline green eyes my way, reddish-brown hair waving over his forehead in stylish disarray. "Izzy?" His gaze roves my body, or what he can see of it above the waist-high countertop, noting The Voltage apron tied around my neck. "You still work here?"

I straighten at the perceived criticism. "What's wrong with that? At least I earn my way, unlike *some* people I won't mention."

It isn't his fault his parents are lawyers and left this dump for a better life, but that doesn't make it any easier to stomach my circumstances.

He raises his hands and takes a step back, as though to protect himself from my toxic attitude. I can't blame him for that, either.

"Hey, it was just a question. It's good to see you again, it's been a while."

Conscious of Jay, I fake a light-hearted shrug, which probably looks as ridiculous as it feels, and tap the order pad with chewed fingernails. "Yeah, well, same old, same old around here. You know how it goes. What can I get you, Kyle, the boss is hovering." I shoot Jay a sidelong glance, letting him know I have it under control, and find him closer than I thought, like any closer and we'd be touching, my back to his front—WTH?

"So, you and Izzy are...?" he asks, all casual curiosity while his arm circles my waist to supposedly check the order book even though he knows, and I know, we're all caught up.

"Friends." Kyle hurries to fill in the blank like a good boy scout, his hand flashing out to shake Jay's man-to-man, and suddenly I get how a mouse feels surrounded by all this testosterone—trapped.

Ducking under Jay's outstretched arm, I get away from the lovefest with a mumbled, "be right back."

Striding toward the storeroom, I try not to look like I'm running, though my feet are practically tripping over themselves to escape. Kyle's home, Renée is back, and my life is once again on the verge of imploding. I wonder if it's possible to disappear. Vanish into a world without pain and death and impossible choices.

Just before slipping into the stockroom, I glance back, unable to leave without memorizing Kyle's face the way it is now instead of the way I saw him last, walking away from me the night I lost my innocence—and my father.

The men are still posturing like two roosters in a henhouse, (I don't remember where I heard the saying but it fits). Jay, with his chin up and hands fisted on the counter pulling off a big, bad, biker dude vibe, Kyle, broader in the shoulder, but with a determined smile on his wholesome, handsome face. For a second, the years melt away and I'm that stupid kid again, thinking I could win the love of the best guy in school. But then I ruined it and he walked out on me. I learned a valuable lesson that night, the only person I can count on is me.

The blonde with expensive taste appears at Kyle's side, a beguiling smile turning full pink lips into guy magnets. Jay all but preens, and Kyle wraps an arm around her waist, drawing her close. I've seen enough and turn on my heel to search for I don't know what in the well-organized storage room. The aroma of coffee beans fills the small area, wafting up from the burlap sacks lining the shelves along the wall. The room's walls are a soothing gray and usually calm my nerves, but not today. I plop onto the chair butted up next to Jay's desk in the corner and take a few deep breaths. It's bad enough Mrs. Bains is making noise about Benjamin, I can't deal with that and Renée, and now Kyle. It's like I hit the trifecta of bad luck bombs. Sometimes it's tough to remember I'm turning twenty in a couple of months, I feel ancient. Flotsam cast on a stormy beach without a will of my own. The only thing I know for sure is that Ben is all I have left and I'm not letting him go without a fight.

CHAPTER SEVEN

RENÉE

The trip to the police station is made in near silence. I suppose I should be grateful I'm not handcuffed, but all I feel is embarrassment as we slowly drive by the crowd, dispersing now the excitement is over, and worry for Simon's grandmother. Mostly worry. The solid thunk of her body hitting the SUV's bumper will live on in my nightmares for years to come.

"Is this going to take very long? I have to deliver lunch home to my family."

The older of the two, the driver, acts as though I haven't spoken, the other officer glances over his thick shoulder and raises a dark brow. "Was it in your vehicle?"

"Yes?"

He shakes his head and faces forward again. "Your car has been confiscated as evidence, Ma'am. I think lunch will be late."

I sink back, my heart fluttering like a wild thing. "Are you *arresting* me?"

"We're taking you in to get your statement," he states, putting an end to my questions.

I stare out the window as the streets stream by, a mix of residential and business, some old, some new, all seeming to mock my captivity. I've watched enough television programs to know I'm on shaky ground. If Mrs. O'Brian is gravely injured—my stomach flip-flops —and the police determine I'm at fault... well, I wouldn't be much help to my family from a jail cell. Nor could I live with the fact I hurt anyone, much less Simon's gentle grandmother.

"Aren't I allowed a phone call?" I stutter, nerves hollowing my insides out. The thought of the spicy burritos I bought from the Mexican place near the highway turns my stomach now, my appetite long gone.

The driver, Officer Bear going by his attitude, if not size, eyes me in the rearview. "This isn't a soap opera. You come in, make your statement official, you go home—simple."

Simple. Easy for him to say. My first day in town and I've already run afoul of my sister and knocked over a senior citizen with my car—oh yeah, and landed my butt in the back of a police cruiser—not an auspicious start.

"When do I get my SUV back?"

Officer Gym (come on, those muscles don't come naturally) sighs as though he's the one having a bad day. He should try my life on for size.

"We'll need it for a few days until our forensics team is done, then you can pay the salvage lot to retrieve it. Shouldn't be more than a week or two." He glances back again and gives me a decidedly evil grin, my horror reflected in his Ray-Bans.

"Two weeks. I can't go without my vehicle for that long. How am I supposed to get around?" The thought of being trapped twenty-four-seven in our house of memories with my sister is enough to consider turning myself over to the police and begging for mercy.

Officer Gym is a pro with the one-arm shoulder shrug. "Same way humans have been doing it for thousands of years, I guess. You walk."

Great, a wise guy.

It's not that I have anything against using my feet, it's more the sense of independence my vehicle gives me. It's the way I got out of this town in the first place.

Mabel has been with me through the hard times—I need her.

The police station comes up on the right, another new addition since I've been gone. It's twice as large as the old building and looks imposing as we pull up near the entry. The parking lot is full of marked cars and even some ghost cruisers, as my sister likes to call them, and there are a few uniformed patrolmen standing near the doors. One, a heavy-set man with jowls and a paunch straining the buttons on his shirt, turns to watch as Officers Gym and Bear climb out, their night-sticks rattling against the door jams. They exchange a few words with the other guy, then Officer Gym opens the back door and ushers me out.

I may not be under arrest, but it sure feels like I'm a felon with the two of them bookending me up the short flight of stairs and straight toward the portal of doom. But just before we disappear into the bowels of the station, jowl guy hollers for us to wait a sec.

Officer Bear huffs one of his put-upon sighs, but brings our cozy little trio to a stop, his hand on my arm gentle, but firm.

"What do you need, Gus?" he asks, his tone impatient.

Gus wanders closer, his eyes narrowed as he takes me in. "Don't I know you from somewhere?"

I glance up sharply, not liking where this is going. "No, I—"

"That's it," he chortles, slapping a hand on his thigh. "You're the kid who found her father the night he offed himself."

The sky tilts, my stomach rising into my throat as his words bring the nightmare I've tried so hard to bury to the forefront of my mind. I'm vaguely aware of Bear wrapping an arm around my shoulders and half-carrying me into the precinct while Gym flexes his muscles and turns into a human wall between me and the prying eyes of Gus and his cronies.

"I'm sorry about that. O'Hare had no business saying such a thing. He *will* be reprimanded—for all the good it will do," Bear adds under his breath, guiding me to a nearby chair. "You're pale, drop your head between your knees." In case I don't comprehend, he helps it along by applying pressure to the back of my skull until I'm folded in half, blinking at the scuffed white tile under my seat.

"Breathe now. In, hold it. Out, hold it. That's right, nice and easy." He releases a relieved breath of his own as blood rushes to my face, making my head swim.

I slowly sit up and eye Officer Bear warily. "Now what?"

"We get your statement and then you go home.

Nothing has changed for me. You?" He ruins his hard-ass persona by handing me a tissue.

"No," I say, patting damp cheeks. "Nothing has changed."

———⊙⌇⊙———

Two hours later the questioning is over, my statement given, and I've been officially released from custody. Rather than calling Izzy for a ride or waiting for a cab, I decide to walk so I can clear my head.

As I exit the building, there's no sign of the officer who accosted me and I can only assume Bear and Gym followed through on their promise to see him brought before his captain. The night my dad took his life is a blur of events, from the argument with Izzy and my boyfriend's betrayal, to the oppressive silence coming from our backyard. Even before I dared to open the gate, I knew something was very wrong.

"Need a lift?"

Startled, I turn to see a familiar face smiling at me from the cab of a sleek red convertible. "Jim?"

"Come on, it hasn't been that long, has it?" He grins, pulling to the side of the curb next to me.

He looks the same with his open, friendly gaze and

messy dark hair. "Two years. How have you been, Jim?"

He shrugs. "Went to college for a bit, decided it wasn't for me, came back, and got a job at the quarry. Money's good, anyway." He runs a hand over his steering wheel. "Come on, get in. I'll take you for a ride —unless you're too busy for old friends?"

He couches the invitation with another smile, but I can see the uncertainty in his eyes. After the breakup with Simon and the stuff with my dad, I backed away from relationships I'd had for years. It felt like anyone who called or came to the door on the pretext of kindness, was only there to place my feelings under a microscope, or find out the salient details, and I couldn't take it, I had to leave before the twisted mass of hurt and anger and sorrow and betrayal swirling in my gut leaked out and gave everyone the show they were looking for.

But I'm better now. A year's worth of counseling and some much-needed distance has given me the tools I need to survive life's curveballs. The secret; compartmentalize.

"Tackle one issue at a time and you'll avoid becoming overwhelmed," Dr. Goodbar stated at one of our weekly meetings. "In times of extreme stress, our brain's cognitive ability slows, allowing emotion to overrule function. It disrupts the regulation of our synapses, resulting in avoidance of interactions with others and a loss of societal tendencies."

"I'm not the best company, it's been a rough morning." I gaze longingly at the luxurious leather seats and try to ignore my aching feet. I hadn't planned on a five-mile walk when I left the house this morning and my heels are killing me.

"All the more reason to come for a drive." He leans across the console and opens the passenger door. "You look like you could use some fun," he coaxes.

Not sure if *fun* is something I should be considering on the eve of my mother's funeral, but Jim has always been kind to me and I need to work on my interactions, so I accept his invitation by sliding in and closing the door before I can talk myself out of it.

"Nice car." I hurry to wrap the seatbelt around my waist as he takes off with a smooth shift of gears. "I never figured you for the sports car type."

He shoots me a sidelong glance before hiding behind the sunglasses he has resting on the dash. "I'm surprised I had a place in your thoughts, what with you and Simon and all."

True enough. Simon does—did—take up a lot of my attention. But that's in the past, though I can't resist digging a little, since Jim brought him up.

"I hear he's getting married." I'm impressed with my casual tone but keep my gaze focused out the windshield so as not to give anything—not that there is anything to give—away. The cherry trees are in full bloom and look spectacular, with pink blossoms drifting around the car to ride wind currents in little tornadoes of color.

"End of summer," Jim acknowledges. "Lacey is… beautiful."

There's a lot he's not saying, and I wonder if she's coming between the childhood friends. "I'm happy for him." And I am, even though my heart pinches at the thought of Simon married. Sharing his life with another woman. A big house filled with love and laughter, anniversaries, kids—he always said we'd have four, two boys and two girls—grandkids…

"What about you?" I ask, desperate to change the subject. "Is there a Mrs. Bailey you want to tell me about?"

He laughs, signaling to turn into the local drive-thru. "Nah, I'm not ready to settle down yet. Besides, you won't have me." He grins to show me he's teasing. "I'm starved, want a burger?"

Surprisingly, my appetite has made a return and I nod, inhaling the greasy goodness coming out of the building's chimney. "Curly fries and a Diet Coke, please, and I'm buying." I dig into my purse, but Jim already has his card out for a quick swipe-and-go, so I smile my thanks and sit back to enjoy my drink.

"You always did love those curly fries. I remember Simon..." Jim hesitates, shooting me a wary look.

"It's fine," I assure him. Simon and I went out for two years and were friends before that. Our lives are interwoven into the fabric of my childhood, and I wouldn't change it even if I could. "He bought me a year's supply for my birthday and you guys thought I'd freak but I loved it—I remember." I take a bite of seasoned deep-fried potato and savor the flavor. "I also remember you warning me it was bad for my cholesterol- you were such a geek," I say fondly.

His neck turns red, but he grins good-naturedly and gobbles down the double-patty-bacon-cheese-extra-mayo-hold-the-lettuce he'd ordered at the window.

"As you can see, I've come over to the dark side." He swipes a napkin from the console and cleans away the evidence, then takes a big swig of strawberry milkshake before stealing one of my fries.

"Hey!" I bat his fingers away. "Get your own."

"What did your momma tell you about sharing?" he teases, then frowns. "Oh, shit, I'm sorry, kid. I heard about your mom from Simon—rough break."

Simon knows my mom died?

"Thanks." I turn my head to look out the side window—and blink back tears. "I should have been here."

He awkwardly pats my shoulder. "She was proud of you, Renée, we all are."

Proud. That just makes it worse, somehow. Instead of being here to support my family in the aftermath of my father's suicide, I'd left them to pursue my own destiny. Not my finest moment. Which is why I'm here, to make restitution.

"Jim, can you take me to the hospital?"

CHAPTER EIGHT

SIMON

I love my job and normally enjoy the time spent at the station with the guys between calls—the paramedics have a bay in the Firehall, which works since most emergencies involve all hands on deck—but today I can't seem to keep my mind on the desultory conversation going on between Dobbs and Fredericks, the fire investigator, that is until they mention the recent fire at the Smuggler's Cove Middle School. A dumpster had been fully engulfed by the time we arrived on scene, dangerously close to a portable used for an extra classroom—thankfully, it was a Saturday and no kids were in the building at the time of the blaze.

"We found an accelerant lodged between the trailer and the dumpster. The fire was set deliberately.

I spoke with the principal, he says there have been other occurrences of mischief in the last few months, but nothing this destructive. A few stolen laptops, graffiti on the walls, that sort of thing."

"Were there signs of forced entry in those instances?" I lean forward to see past Dobbs, who's gobbling up the leftover chili.

Fredericks shakes his head and pushes up wire-framed glasses under salt and pepper brows. "No, which leaves me to wonder if it was negligence or something more?"

"Did they call the police, set up an investigation?"

Fredericks shrugs. "Not sure, but they're involved now. Arson is a serious matter."

"So, you don't think it was an accident? A way to keep warm, maybe? We have a homelessness issue in Smuggler's Cove."

"Yeah, and I'm going to be one of them myself if Doreen doesn't get an invitation to your wedding soon." Dobbs waves a thick crust of homemade bread slathered in butter at my face. "You're killing me, man."

Dammit, Lacey promised to send RSVPs to all my friends a month ago and she still hasn't. I have a feeling she doesn't plan on having them at her wedding. That's how I've come to think of it; *her* wedding. I'm just along for the ride.

"Sorry, buddy. Lacey has a lot on her mind. I'll

remind her tonight. You've gotta be there, we're partners, aren't we?"

"That's what I keep telling the ol' lady, but you know how they are—any excuse to spend dough on a new dress and a hairdo."

He talks tough, but I happen to know Dobbs adores his wife of twenty-five years. The couple has been through some rough times, including the loss of their son in a horrific car accident, so it's no wonder he's protective. If Lacey doesn't send the invite tonight, I will. It's just one more thing about this wedding I don't like. I've tried to stay out of the way and let my bride-to-be run the show—after all, women plan their big day from the time they're girls, don't they?—but hell, it's my wedding, too.

"I'm more interested in seeing *you* in a suit," I tell him to lighten the atmosphere. "Do they even come in your size?" He weighs something like one-twenty soaking wet, but I like to rib the guy whenever I get the chance, 'cause he eats constantly, like twenty-four-seven. I don't know where he sticks it all—well, yes I do. When he's not filling his trap with food, he's using it to gab. The guy is a regular chatterbox. If it's not world events (enough fodder for months there), it's his family, or sports—don't get him going on the WarHawks hockey team, he'll relay every player's stat, position, time they spend in the john, you name it, he knows it.

"You'll be too busy gawking at your beautiful bride to notice anyone else in the room, trust me." He swipes at the crumbs on his pants, then pushes his chair back, carries his dishes to the waiting sink, and gives them a rinse.

"Mind if we get back to the topic at hand?" Fredericks asks, his forehead a country road of creases and crevices. "The captain is getting pressured for answers, the mayor's kids attend that school."

Never mind all the hard-working families whose children also attend Smuggler's Cove Middle School. I keep my cynicism to myself and cross my arms over my chest, leaning the chair back on two legs, a habit I've had since *I* was in middle school. "Is there any CCTV footage in the area? Someone must have seen something."

Fredericks shakes his head. "Nah, there's a park across the street, and other than that it's all residential. We have officers going door-to-door looking for dash cam recordings, but nothing so far. The guy's a ghost."

"What makes you think it's a male?"

"Ninety percent of arsonists are white males," Frederick states, tapping a silver pen against the edge of the table.

"Doesn't say much for our gender, does it?" I let my chair drop to all fours with a bang. "Wish there was something I could tell you, but by the time we arrived on scene the crew had the fire under control."

"Notice anyone hanging around? Someone who looked suspicious, maybe?"

Dobbs throws the towel he used to dry his hands on the counter. "Look, we were there to care for injuries, we aren't the cops." He comes over and clasps my shoulder. "Shift's over, kid. You should head out and check on your grandmother, I'll handle the paperwork. It's my turn."

My pulse kicks up a beat, concern for Grams warring with the memory of seeing Renée. After I make sure Grandma is comfortable, I'll run over to the police station. She must be freaking out. The police were rough on her after her dad died. I tried to be there for her then, too, but she wouldn't have anything to do with me. Maybe, it will be the same today.

I should stay away, but know I won't.

GRANDMA'S FAVORITE FLOWERS, DAISIES, ARE IN the hospital gift shop in a cute teddy bear vase. It reminds me of the dandelions I picked for her as a kid. She'd placed them in a china teacup covered in pink roses and declared them the loveliest gift she'd ever received. With Dad working two jobs and Mom waitressing for long hours, Grandma was the only stability I had as a child. Thinking of her in that hospital bed put a knot in my gut.

I hurry to pay for the bouquet, and seeing the busy elevators, take the stairs to the fourth floor, the ceramic vase cool in my hand. A nurse with dark hair held back in a tight bun looks up and smiles as the heavy metal door closes with a clang.

"Oh, those are pretty," she says, her gaze sweeping my face before taking in the uniform and the flowers. "For a patient, I presume?"

I nod, feeling silly. I should have bought something elegant, roses or lilies maybe. "My grandmother, Katherine O'Brian, was admitted this morning."

She gives me a sympathetic look, then taps a few keys on the keyboard, and waits a moment for the results, before pointing down the long hall on my right. "They just brought her back from x-rays, so she may be tired, but you're welcome to stop in and check on her. She's in room 411, just down the hall. Visiting hours begin at nine a.m. and end at seven p.m. The doctor should be around shortly if you have any questions."

"Thanks." I'm already turning away almost before she's done giving directions. The sooner I see how Grams is doing, the better I'll feel.

The murmur of voices coming through a partially closed door guides me to the right room. I hesitate, my nerves getting the best of me now that I'm here. The doctor must be in with Grandma now and I debate whether I should interrupt the exam. Even though I'm trained in patient care, this is different—it's family.

Taking a deep breath, I rap my knuckles lightly on the door before pushing it wide, then freeze, my heart taking flight like a caged bird. Instead of old Dr. Dunsmuir with his requisite stethoscope, a golden angel sits at my grandmother's bedside.

"What are you doing here?" I force leaden feet across the floor, antagonism making my tone sharp.

"Simon," Grandma warns, well aware of my caged resentment. "It was kind of your young lady to keep me company."

"Not mine, not anymore. Isn't that right, Renée?" I should feel satisfaction at the pain darkening her beautiful blue eyes, but shame for my attitude when she just lost her mother steals the heat from my anger.

I bend to kiss Grams' papery cheek and grimace at the black and blue bruises coloring her shoulder and arm lying on top of the white coverlet. "How do you feel?"

She smiles. "Like I was hit by a bus."

Renée squeezes her fingers. "I can't believe you're taking this so well. If it was me, I wouldn't be so forgiving. Is there anything I can get for you?"

Grandma gives a delicate shiver. "Would you mind tracking down that sweet nurse and asking for another heated blanket? I can't seem to get warm."

"Of course!" Renée jumps to her feet, spares me a glance from under moon-dipped lashes, then hurries from the room, the door closing gently behind her.

I raise my brow, setting the vase on Grams' bedside table before taking a seat. "What was that about? You know very well if you ring the buzzer hanging right there by your hand the staff would come running."

"Shh now, we don't have much time." She gives me back a raised brow and throws in a pinch to get my attention. "So, how are you going to get that girl back?"

"Ow," I grumble, rubbing the sore spot on my arm. "There is no getting her back. Renée decided a long time ago that our relationship was over, not me. Besides, she just about ran you over, remember?"

"Oh, tch. It's not as though she aimed for me, it was an accident. And as to the other... I taught you better than to give up the moment things get tough. Is she worth it, or not?"

Grams stares at me with faded blue eyes that see too much. Her dementia has affected her natural reticence and brought out the inner bully, it seems. She asked an insightful question though; one I've been asking myself since Renée reappeared in my life. Is it worth ending my relationship with Lacey and our marriage to try and rekindle the past? Something tells me it would be a mistake. Renée isn't going to stick around and I'm not ready to leave even if she asks. There's too much water under the bridge between us, it's best to leave it submerged.

"I'm getting married soon, Grams. Lacey is a good person. We suit each other." I fiddle with the side rail on her bed, unwilling to meet her knowing gaze.

"You're running scared. You know it, I know it, and soon, your bride-to-be will know it, too. You can't hide from love, Simon. It seeps through the pores and fills your soul until it leaks out like the sun's rays, spreading warmth everywhere you go. Do you really want to give that up?" She grasps my fingers and squeezes, the wedding band she never removed, though Grandpa has been gone twenty-some years, glinting on her hand.

"Grams, I'm..." Confused. Terrified. *Captivated* is all I can think, my heart skipping a beat, as Renée reenters the room followed by the friendly nurse from the station desk and Dr. Dunsmuir.

"Well, I'm glad to see your color improving, my dear." Dr. Dunsmuir gives me a nod as I rise and move a few steps back to allow the nurse to check Grandma's vitals after covering her with the requested blanket. "Must be the company you're keeping." He winks at Renée, the old codger.

She gifts him with a shy smile before looking at me and lifting her chin. No sign of the smile now, I notice.

"Dr. Dunsmuir has a suggestion and I think it's a good idea." Renée turns to Grams. "You're going to need someone to help around your home for a couple of weeks until you're fully recovered from the *accident*," she stresses with another glance in my direction. "If you're willing, I'd like to accept the position. I can cook fairly well, clean your house, and generally be there for whatever you need. I promise not to disrupt your routine or anything," she hurries to add, which in turn makes me wonder why she seems to want this so badly.

"Shouldn't you be spending time with your own family?" I frown and cross my arms. Dunsmuir is right, Grams *should* have homecare, but not my ex-girlfriend. She's not even a nurse, for Pete's sake.

"Simon, manners don't go out the window just because you're an adult," She chastises to my utter embarrassment. Her eyelids flutter as though she's making a wish—or dreaming up ways to teach me some etiquette—before opening them and bestowing a warm smile on Renée. "I'm sorry for my grandson's rude behavior, he loves me you see, and his emotions tend to get away from him when he's worried. I would probably be fine on my own, but, if it makes the doctor happy..." She gives him a coquettish sidelong glance, "then I can hardly turn down your kind offer. That house is too big for one old woman, anyway."

She holds out her hands and waits until I take one and Renée grasps the other from the opposite side of the bed. "Now then, you two are going to be seeing a fair amount of each other, what with Simon renting the room over the garage and all, so I expect you to play nice with one another—understand?"

Renée's eyes widen comically. "But... if he's already on the property..."

I hide my grin, suddenly getting some enjoyment out of the impending situation. "Ahh, but I have a job, remember? I put in long hours and can't always find the time to check on Grams." No need to tell her we share dinner every Sunday night, she'll find out soon enough.

Doctor Dunsmuir claps his hands. "Now we have that settled, I'd like to book you for a few more tests, including an MRI, and then we'll make arrangements with this young lady about your home care routine and health regimen. She tells me she has a Master of

Science in physical therapy with a minor in physiotherapy, so this is a match made in heaven. Right, Simon?"

So that's what she'd left him for—a degree. Did she assume he'd hold her back? Expect a stay-at-home wife and basketball team worth of kids? She didn't know him at all.

"Yeah, sure. A real pair."

CHAPTER NINE

RENÉE

I make an excuse to leave the hospital room as soon as possible and promise Mrs. O'Brian I'll meet her at her home when she is released. For now, I need to put some space between me and Simon and the impossible situation we've landed ourselves in.

"Renée, hold up."

My pulse leaps and I hesitate, my fingers hovering over the rows of buttons in the empty elevator. Simon is striding toward me, a determined glint in his eyes. He's still in uniform, the dark shirt outlining muscular shoulders, the sharply creased slacks, lean hips, and long legs. He was tall in high school, with a body the girls drooled over, but now... now he's so much more. Intriguing, intimidating, intense, and I'm suddenly afraid my infatuation for this man will once again leave me heartbroken.

"Sorry, I'm in a hurry," I mumble, stabbing the *close door* button repeatedly and praying he trips in oversized black leather boots that lend him a dangerous air.

"Too much of a hurry for me but not for Jim, is that it?" His size twelve is a more than adequate wedge, stopping the sliding door just as it's about to close. He ambles into the suddenly shrinking steel box and reaches past me—his arm brushing my breast causing me to leap away like a scalded cat—and gently taps the first-floor button before stepping back to lean against the far wall in a GQ pose worthy of the next firefighter's calendar.

"J... Jim was nice enough to offer me a ride after my car was impounded," I stutter. "Not that it's any of *your* business." At least I know not to spill any family secrets to Traitor Jim, obviously, their Bro-Code is still in play.

The elevator slows and I sigh my relief until I glance up and see we're on the second floor. The doors whoosh open and a group of three—a frail-looking woman standing next to an equally diminished man in a wheelchair, and another man, a younger version of the two of them with white-knuckled hands gripping the handles—join us, forcing Simon into my corner. He tucks himself behind me, the heat from his body warming me from shoulder to thigh. And then the elevator hiccups into motion and his hand sears my waist. I freeze, the familiarity of his touch sweeping over me in a tumultuous tide. He'd introduced me to the hypnotic lure of passion and all the many ways there are to tease and torture a body into ecstasy as an impressionable sophomore. I fell headlong in love, but, for Simon, it was all a game.

I jerk free, my gaze on the descending floor numbers, willing them to hurry and release me from this torment. The elevator is silent other than the creaks and groans of the wheelchair, and intermittent beeps from the IV bag attached to the side of the chair. Finally, we reach the main level and the doors swish open, spilling us into a busy corridor. The family slowly wanders toward the cafeteria, the elderly woman gripping her husband's shoulder, a plain brown purse over her opposite arm, and the son hovering protectively over his parents.

Exhaling, I dodge a couple of RNs and stride past the atrium, ignoring the footsteps keeping time with mine.

"Jeff tells me you're not seeing anyone." Simon nods to the reception staff and gets flirty smiles in return. "Is that true?" He grasps my elbow in a firm grip and leads me through the sliding glass doors.

Once again, I break free, sparks from his touch racing through my bloodstream. "Quit manhandling me, Simon," I snap, full of virtuous resentment. "You lost the right to ask me personal questions a long time ago. If that's going to be a problem, your grandmother can hire someone else to help with her care."

His brows furrow and he cocks his head. "Where is all this animosity coming from? You left me, remember?"

I gasp, stunned by his callousness. "You're kidding, right? I am *not* going down that road with you. Whatever happened is in the past. You're about to get married!" My voice echoes off the cement walls, startling patients and their families in the rotunda.

A dark flush stains his cheeks, but he nods. "Look, can we talk for a minute?" He points to a bench set away from the walk in a small courtyard, the late afternoon sun leaving it mostly in shadow.

I would much rather march off in righteous indignation, but we are bound to run into each other even if I decide not to work with his grandmother, so I reluctantly trudge to the utilitarian bench painted a bright waxy white, and take a seat, hugging my shoulder bag to my chest.

"I'm not sure what there is to say," I begin, then stumble to a stop when he sinks down beside me and slides an arm along the backrest, inches from my shoulders.

"You look good, Renée," he murmurs, his rich baritone sending quivers like a tuning fork on my spine. "I thought of you often after you left without a word. I even stopped by to get a forwarding address from your mom, but your sister told me you were done with me." He gently brushes hair behind my ear, and I give an involuntary shiver. "What happened to us, huh? I thought we were getting serious, and then, suddenly, you were gone."

The urge to blurt the whole nightmarish truth burns my throat, but what would it achieve? We're two different people from those innocent kids. I need to make amends to my family, and Simon is starting one— with another woman.

I shake my head, tears close to the surface. "It doesn't matter, it's over and done. I'm only here until after Mom's funeral and then I'll be heading back to... home. I'm planning to start my physiotherapy clinic and have a lot to get completed before opening."

I can feel him staring at me but refuse to meet his gaze. "I should go. Izzy is probably wondering what happened to her lunch."

I rise and prepare to leave him behind, though my heart pinches at the thought, but he snatches my hand, tugging me around to face him.

"What about Grams? You promised her." He looks up, his eyes pleading. "She needs you, Renée. *I* need you."

Oh, God. How am I supposed to walk away from that? Even though I know it's a bad idea, and nothing good can come of it, I give in to his request. "I can stay until the end of summer, but I'm doing this for your grandmother—no other reason."

He brushes my knuckles with his lips, his breath a soft sigh over my skin. "Of course."

I tug my hand away, my stomach clenching. What have I done?

CHAPTER TEN

IZZY

The water is cooling in the kitchen sink and my fingers are prunes. Instead of doing the dinner dishes, I've been staring out the window as though willpower alone will bring my sister home. I should know better, she's a runner, it's what she does. Ever since we were kids, if things got rough, she would take off and hide in the backyard—mostly in the ramshackle treehouse built supposedly for both of us, but mostly for Renée. Even then I knew she was different; quieter, more introspective. She might be the eldest by a year and ten months, but I'm the caregiver in the family.

A fork clatters onto a plate behind me and I glance over my shoulder, taking in the dark cloud hovering over my brother's head. He's hunched over the plate, elbows on the table, and too-long bangs hiding his eyes. The homework I'd warned him had to be done by the end of the weekend sits stacked to the side, not even opened.

I sigh and turn to lean against the cabinet, drying wet hands with Mom's faded old dishtowel while trying to decide how far to push him. "Hey, bud, if you're done can you bring me your plate? I'd like to get these dishes done before midnight." My pitiful attempt at levity falls on deaf ears, he doesn't even twitch.

"Benjamin."

I throw the towel at his head and grin as it baffs him in the ear before sliding to the floor. My smile dies a slow death when he looks up and shoots me the finger. *What the hell?* Where did my happy-go-lucky little brother disappear to? I get things have been tough, what with Mom dying, but I'm doing the best I can here. We were brought up to respect not just our elders but one another, as well. His morose attitude lately is wearing on my nerves.

"Not cool. What's your problem?" I straighten and stride over to pick up the discarded towel and his dish, nudging the books with my arm. "You better get started, there's a lot to do."

"I don't feel like it," he mutters, pushing back from the table, his chair scraping noisily across the linoleum. "I'm going to my room."

"Not so fast, mister." I step into his path, forcing him to stay put for a minute. "We need to talk."

"About what? I didn't do anything." He glares at me from beneath the waterfall of his bangs.

He's the same height as me now, and bulkier. I'm not afraid of him, he's my brother. But it would be prudent to deescalate his antagonism before he closes down completely, though if he didn't do anything there shouldn't be any reason to get so aggressive. A worrying thought for later reflection.

"We have a scheduled meeting with Mrs. Bains tomorrow morning. I need you to get a good night's sleep and keep quiet about Renée being in town, okay?"

He gazes at me suspiciously. "Why would we lie? And besides, she hasn't been here all day. I bet you've already scared her off."

"First, it's not lying, it's omitting—big difference. And second, she hasn't been home in almost two years, I'm sure she just got caught up with old acquaintances. Don't worry, Renée will be here soon." Who am I trying to convince? On one hand, it would be easier if she'd stayed away. At least I wouldn't feel these tendrils of hope ballooning in my chest while waiting for the inevitable pin.

"I still don't get why it matters if the Bain Brain knows my big sister is in town." He crosses his arms and stares me down, arrogance seeping from his pores.

I suck in a pained breath and slowly exhale. I don't know why he's picking a fight but it's not like him. Much as I love him, I'm not sure I can fix whatever is going on with him, and that scares the hell out of me.

Forcing a calmness I'm far from feeling, I give a slight shrug. "I just want to give it a few days before we throw a Welcome Home, Renée, Party, that's all. Now, as your *other* big sister, you have homework to do, so get busy. The sooner it gets done, the sooner I can get off your back about it."

"Bite m—" His delighted agreement (yeah, right) is cut off by the deep roar of a supercharged engine coming down the street.

It's a tie between Ben and me for who reaches the front door first, but my hand is firm on the knob. "It's probably Jay. No more excuses, get back to work." Jay owns a Harley and it has a meaty sound, but something tells me Renée has finally shown up. The question is, who brought her home, and why?

He scowls and trudges down the hall, resentment in every line of his gangly body.

When I'm sure he's gone, I tug the door open and peer into the deepening twilight shadows at a Barracuda parked under the pine tree in front of the house. The passenger door opens and the car's interior light blinks on, highlighting the two people in the front seats. What is Renée doing with Simon Fraser? Word at The Voltage is that he's getting married soon, the last thing he needs is our family's drama in his life again.

"Renée, you're home!" Benjamin races around the side of the house, the back gate clanging like a warning bell behind him.

I step onto the porch to stop him, but it's too late, he's already in the front yard, his steps slowing as he nears the sports car.

Renée gets out and rounds the hood in a rush, tears streaking her cheeks. "Ben," she cries, throwing herself into his arms. They stand like that for a long moment and my throat tightens. I'm on the outside looking in, but, for once, I don't mind. We were so close, the three of us, back before the loss of our parents—and nothing has been the same since.

Simon climbs out from behind the wheel of his car and sends me an uncertain smile. "Izzy."

"Simon. Thanks for bringing my sister home. Did her old wreck give up the ghost?" He comes to the coffee shop now and then with his emergency services team-mates, or Marv and Jim, his school chums. We aren't exactly friends—he's nearly five years older—more like acquaintances who know each other's dirty little secrets.

"Not quite," Renée answers, her arm around

Benjamin's waist. They're the same height, and I wonder if she's as startled as I am by the amount he's grown. Our little brother isn't a baby anymore. I would be wise to heed the changes or risk alienating him more than I've already done.

"I better get going," Simon says, an arm folded on the roof of his car and a foot resting on the door jam. The breeze teases his hair and molds the dark shirt he's wearing to his muscular chest. He was a good-looking boy who has since turned into an Adonis with beguiling dimples. It's no surprise my sister was—and maybe, still is— infatuated with him.

"Thanks again for the ride." Renée lifts her chin and a blush of pink stains her cheeks. "Will I see you tomorrow?"

See him tomorrow? What does that mean? Does she think she can pick up where she left off before running away? It's just like Renée to expect the world to revolve around her. I wait for Simon to disabuse her of the notion, a smirk on my lips, only to gasp at his reply.

"I won't be home until dinner, but I'll try to drop in. Call me if you have any problems. Do you have my number?"

She hesitates, then nods, shooting me a glance. Tough. I have a right to know she plans to ruin our family's already shaky reputation by going after an unavailable man.

I open my mouth to state my opinion of their ill-advised reunion, but Simon is already climbing into his car after lifting his hand in a salute, so I wait until the rumble of his vehicle fades down the street before rounding on my sister.

"Are you crazy? You do know he's engaged, right? To the mayor's daughter, Renée. You can't just come back here and..."

"Stop it," Benjamin shouts, stomping his foot for emphasis. "You're not our mother, so quit bossing us around. You're going to ruin everything. I wish you weren't my sister." He breaks away from Renée and sprints for the house, leaving my heart ripped open and bleeding on the ground beneath his feet.

"He didn't mean it," Renée says quietly, handing me a tissue.

I stare at her blankly, then slowly shake my head. "I hope not," I whisper, not at all sure she's right.

"It's not what you're thinking, with Simon." She carefully blots the tears I wasn't aware of shedding from my face. "I'm going to help his grandmother with her physiotherapy and homecare for a couple of weeks. I would have told you and Ben tonight, but, well..." She shrugs and offers a wan smile.

"What's wrong with Simon's grandmother?" She

and Doc Dunsmuir are regulars at the coffee shop and seem like such a cute couple.

"I hit her with my car today."

I stare at my sister, shocked. "You what?"

"It was an accident," she hurries to assure me, twisting the tissue to shreds. "I looked away for just a second and she stepped off the curb—I still can't believe it."

"How bad, Renée? Can she walk?" I grasp her arms and give them a shake. "My God, you could have killed her!"

She stares at me, stricken. "Do you think I don't realize that, Izzy? I spent most of the day sitting in a police interrogation room. They confiscated my car, for cripes sake." She twists away and rubs the red marks I've left on her skin. "I went to the hospital as soon as I was released. She's going to be okay but needs extra care for a while. It's the least I can do."

Simon's comments make more sense now. Instead of destroying his upcoming marriage, as I'd assumed, she's decided to bring the family name into the spotlight with a hit-and-almost-run of one of the town's most loved seniors—just great.

"I can't believe you knocked her down. Nice way to catch your old boyfriend's attention. I'm guessing he was the one to respond to the call?" He'd been in his uniform when he dropped her off, so it wasn't much of a stretch considering Smuggler's Cove only has two ambulances.

"He looks good, doesn't he?"

The melancholy tone of her voice worries me. "Renée, listen to me. Simon has moved on. He has a fiancée and a career he seems to enjoy. Don't do anything stupid, okay? It's too late for regrets. You need to let him go."

She nods, her eyes infinitely sad. "I know, but what if I can't?"

Then we're all in trouble.

CHAPTER ELEVEN

SIMON

I push the heavy wood door to Suds and Buds and enter the bar, quiet on a Monday night. I should be home catching up with the sleep I've missed out on while working twelve-hour shifts but am too wound up for rest.

Jim and Marv lift their bottles in greeting from our regular table near the stage where a young woman is sitting on a stool under a wedge of light strumming a beat-up guitar. She's not bad if you like soft, croony tunes, but I can tell Marv's been giving her a hard time by the bright spots of pink on her cheeks, and the way she's angled away from the guys.

"If it isn't rap, it must be crap." I can practically hear Marv tormenting the poor girl. He's a lost cause when it comes to flirting. He has no filter and generally spits out whatever he's thinking. On the plus side, you always know where you stand with the guy.

Lisa, Lacey's best friend, gives me a wave from behind the bar and points to the draft with a raised brow. I smile and nod, then wind my way to my buddies.

"Drinking tonight? You must be done saving lives for a day or two, Superman." Jim gives a sloppy grin, then stands to clap my back before retaking his seat none too steadily.

"Looks as though you already have a head start," I retort, sinking into a bar chair with a tired sigh.

"Tough shift?" Marv asks, eyeing Lisa as she arrives with an icy glass of foaming honey-gold craft, and two more bottles of beer on a tray. She expertly plucks the empties off the table, gives it a swipe with a snowy white cloth scented with bleach, and sets the new drinks on coasters with the Suds and Buds logo—three guys swimming in a vat of beer. Ironic considering how many times we drank each other under the table in this bar. I even met Lacey here.

"You mean loudmouth hasn't spilled the beans yet?" I thank Lisa and watch her slowly return to the bar, her ears practically twitching. I know she tells Lacey everything she hears, and I don't plan on being in any more crap than I'm already facing when Lace finds out my ex-girlfriend is going to be my neighbor. A chill creeps down my neck and I scrub it away.

"I'd tap that," Marv mutters around the mouth of his sweating beer bottle, gaze unwavering on the pretty barmaid. "What beans?" he adds belatedly.

"You don't stand a chance, Bro. She has too much class for the likes of you. Now me?" Jim bangs his narrow chest with a cocky grin. "I'd have to fight her off this hot bod."

"In your dreams, Bailey. She's never given you the time of day." Marv leans his chair back on two legs and turns his attention to me. "Jimbo's been bragging about taking Renée Thomas out for a pleasure cruise to show off his new ride, but I figured it for bullshit. Renée washed all of us off her lily-white hands years ago. She ain't here—*is she?*"

Something about my expression gives me away because he drops the chair to all-fours and slams his bottle on the table, ignoring the foam that erupts from the top and spills down the side and over his fingers. "Are you *shittin'* me? Why? She better not cause trouble for you and Lacey or I'll..."

"Relax. Renée has no interest in picking up where we left off." I ignore the ache in the pit of my stomach to nudge Marv's foot. "What is it with you and her, anyway? You've always had it in for Renée."

Jim snickers. "He's wanted to have *it* in her ever since we were old enough to notice tits, right, *buddy*?"

"Shut your mouth, asshole," Marv snarls, drawing a flat note from the singer's guitar.

I sit back, shocked. "Is that true? You had a thing for my girlfriend?" I can't help it, my hands close into fists, ready to pummel his ugly face into the table.

Marv eyes the clenched knuckles, then slowly raises his gaze to meet the barely leashed anger radiating from mine. "Ex-girlfriend. And as long as you're over her, then yes," he admits. "Hell, we weren't blind, man. Renée was, and probably still is, a babe. But she was yours, off-limits. I was rude to her because I didn't want her friendship—I still don't."

I don't know what to do with this information. Renée is a free agent. She can choose whoever she likes, but... "Do you plan on asking her out?"

Marv shrugs as though it doesn't matter, but his eyes flare. "Not sure if it would be worth my time, though she did accept a ride from *this* never-do-well." He lifts a square jaw toward the slouching Jim, who perks up with a lopsided grin. "Would it be cool with you? I mean, if you still have feelings—"

I swivel in my seat, pulse-pounding, sure that Lisa must be practically breathing over my shoulder. But no, she's delivering drinks on the other side of the room to a table of businessmen dressed in suits and ties. My heartbeat should be settling, but it seems to have lodged in my craw because I'm about to lie to my best friend.

"Renée is seeing someone in Berkeley—sounds serious. She's here for her mother's funeral and then she'll be gone. I wouldn't waste your time on her, she's a flight risk." I duck my head and reach for my beer, but not before noticing Jim's raised eyebrow. Damn, did Renée tell him about my grandmother? Even so, he couldn't know about our arrangement, it happened after he'd seen her. Maybe I'm overthinking it, and maybe Renée does have a guy in her life. Why not? She's smart, kind, caring, and heart-stoppingly gorgeous. I have a sinking feeling this summer is going to be a train wreck.

"Well, a guy can dream, right? I think I'll pay her a visit. It's been a while, we have some catching up to do."

Before I can explain Renée's new lodgings around the gravel pit in my gut, a tingling between my shoulder blades warns us we're about to have company. A glance at Jim confirms who it is—Lacey.

I push my chair back and rise, shooting him a don't-make-trouble glare. The happy-go-lucky drunk of the evening has transformed into a cold, sullen, S.O.B. with attitude.

"There you are." Lace glides up to the table in sky-high heels and a skintight midnight blue dress that doesn't leave much to the imagination. And now I'm comparing my fiancée's dress choices to my ex's—and Lacey is coming up short, dammit. I need to get my head on straight before I blow our relationship.

With that in mind, I'm more effusive than normal and pull her into my arms for a heated kiss. Her start of surprise quickly turns to a throaty moan of need, her sharp nails embedding themselves into my back as the bar explodes into whoops and applause.

"Get a room, you two lovebirds," Lisa chirps from nearby. I lift my head, smile into beautiful cerulean eyes, and wish they were cobalt instead. Damn Renée, why did she have to come back—especially now?

"Better watch out, bro, she's tightening her net around you." Jim makes googly eyes and waves his hands in the air.

Lacey pointedly ignores him to drop gracefully into my chair. Her long legs cross at the knee as she reaches for my glass of beer, leaving me to pull one up for Lisa, who seems to be done for the night, and one that I set between the combatants.

I weave my fingers with Lacey's, the diamond ring I spent two months paying for glinting off the stage lights. "I thought you were going out with your family tonight?" I try not to mind her showing up like this, but I won't deny it's irritating.

"Hmm?" she murmurs, her attention on Lisa chatting it up with Marv. "I hope *he* isn't making a move on my bestie—he's not her type."

I raise my brow. "She's old enough to make her own choices. Besides, Marv's a good guy."

The singer seems to sense the rising tension, or maybe it's the growing crowd and changes up her soft melodies for a stripped-down version of "Takin' Care of Business", a Bachman-Turner Overdrive mega-hit.

A couple of forty-somethings get up and spin around the dance floor, the woman's flats barely touching the scuffed wood, her smile lighting the room. Another couple rise, then another and another, creating a rainbow of swirling bodies.

I lean close to Lacey and keep my voice low. "Are you here to check up on me?"

She tips her head and frowns, but I notice she won't meet my gaze. "Of course not. Lisa called and invited me down for a drink—girls' night out." She smiles and rubs my thigh.

I grasp her hand before it moves higher, not amused. "Trust is a two-way street, sweetheart. If we're going to last, we need to be honest with one another."

She flounces back in her seat, a well-practiced pout making a bow out of her pink lips. "Really? Then what is this I hear about you and another blonde sitting outside the hospital all cozy-like. Want to explain that, *my love?*"

Jim chuckles, his eyes glittering. "Maybe it was the ghost of girlfriend's past, hey, buddy?" His gaze moves from a glowering Lacey to me, and then to the door beyond and the chuckle becomes all-out laughter. "Or maybe, it wasn't a specter at all."

I turn with a sinking feeling in my gut. Sure enough, Renée and her sister have entered the bar like bad luck pennies, and for the first time, I contemplate childishly pulling the nearby fire alarm.

CHAPTER TWELVE

RENÉE

I reluctantly follow my sister into Buds and Suds, wondering how much longer before this never-ending day is over.

She glances over her shoulder, the mini-diamond stud on her nose twinkling, then points toward the bar. I nod and head to an empty table to wait. She dragged me in here, she can buy the first round. After learning about the accident and my time at the police station she decided we should go for a drink—and since I pretty much fouled up our reunion, I agreed. Besides, we need to talk about Benjamin, and I don't want him overhearing what's said.

There's a young woman playing guitar and singing on the stage and couples taking advantage of the quiet bar to kick up their feet on the dance floor. I haven't recognized anyone yet and my shoulders slowly relax—maybe this won't be so bad.

Izzy arrives with a couple of cocktails and slips into a seat, her leather miniskirt sliding north of mid-thigh. When did her taste in clothes change so drastically? It was almost impossible to get her out of jeans and over-sized T-shirts when we were younger. Though the goth-look works with her peaches-and-cream complexion and flame-colored hair. She's grown into a beautiful young woman, Mom and Dad would have been proud.

I take a sip of my drink to clear my throat and come away sputtering. "There's no mix in this."

Izzy grins. "If you're going to have a drink, what's the sense in watering it down?"

I wipe my streaming eyes with a cocktail napkin. "You could have warned me."

"What's the fun in that?" She crosses her legs and lets a chunky black leather boot full of zippers and laces rock back and forth to the music. "This is nice, the Thomas sisters together again."

"I can't say I ever pictured the two of us bar-hopping." And why does she look so comfortable in this setting?

She shrugs and takes another drink of the whiskey, closing her eyes as though to savor the fiery tang on her tongue. "Hardly bar-hopping. We're out for a nightcap and then I need to get back before Ben goes to sleep, I don't like to leave him alone for too long. I'm not a kid anymore, Renée. I have you to thank for dragging me into the world of responsible adults, so don't look down your nose because I like a drink now and then." She drops her foot to the floor, smacks the tumbler onto the table, and glares at the dancers.

I grimace because she's right. I walked out on my family when they needed me the most and I'm not sure I can ever repair the damage.

"Can we start again?" I reach over and squeeze her arm. "I'm Renée Thomas. Do you come here often?"

Izzy's frown slowly turns into a smirk, and she goes back to the metronome thing with her leg. "You're weird. Is the air too thin at that fancy-assed university you've been attending?"

I laugh, attracting the attention of a group of businessmen sitting nearby. A guy with classic features wearing a navy pinstripe suit with a powder blue button-down raises a brow and leans back for a better look. Izzy, the extrovert, notices and gives a salute, the ice in her glass clinking.

"If they come over, I'm out of here," I sputter, taking a fortifying drink of the rye with barely a shiver this time.

"If they come over, we're going to ask them to

dance. Don't be such a Debbie Downer." Izz gives pinstripe guy a wink, then turns her gaze over the sparse crowd.

"Were you expecting someone?" It would explain why she'd been adamant we come out to reconnect tonight.

Her gaze meets mine and bounces away, and suddenly I know—Simon. I no sooner think it, and there he is, leading his girlfriend onto the dance floor. My stomach clenches against the blow of seeing them together; the power couple of Smuggler's Cove, Washington.

"Shit. I'm sorry, Renée. I didn't think *she'd* be here."

She is everything I'm not; beautiful, self-assured, and confident. Secure in the love of a good man. With the hindsight of time, I realized I should have confronted Simon that night. Instead, I jumped to conclusions and never even gave him a chance—or my trust. The girl I was didn't deserve a guy like him, and now... it's too late.

"It doesn't matter. I'm over Simon Fraser." *Liar, liar.* "You're matchmaking skills need work, though," I tease, trying to act like I'm not bleeding from the inside out.

She gives me a perceptive look but lets the matter drop. "Yeah, well, I say screw 'em all, let's dance."

My mouth drops. "You and me?" Never mind the fact we're bound to run into the wonder couple out there.

Izzy stands up and gives her hips a little shimmy. "Why not? We used to jazz it up in the basement as kids, at least until Mom yelled at us to shut down the music." A shadow passes over her fine features before she shakes it off. "C'mon, are you scared?"

I send a panicked glance to the dance floor, only marginally relieved to see Simon on the opposite side, near the stage.

"Petrified," I admit, rising. "You better not step on my toes, or else..."

Izzy laughs and spins away, her lithe body swaying to the music, arms waving over her head. She looks young and joyful when I know life has been challenging the last few years. I envy her ability to compartmentalize like that. I've always been one to get mired down in my emotions. It's one of the reasons I focused my studies on psychology. I'm terrified my dad's genes live on in me.

"Would you like to dance?"

Startled, I turn and find pinstripe guy by my side, smiling as though I couldn't possibly say no. He's wrong.

"Sorry, I have a date." My gaze returns to my tough-as-nails sister, her steps slowing, the laughter fading as she waits for me to turn my back once again. Not happening.

"Excuse me," I say, leaving him behind to join the dancing couples. I don't have the smooth moves Izzy has, but manage a fairly successful version of The Sprinkler, which earns me a clear path to her side.

"Don't ever do that again," she mutters, glaring at the people giving us sideway glances as they swing past.

"Do what?" I retort. "This?" I repeat the 90's dance move, circling her like an elephant at a watering hole. "I told you I couldn't dance."

"Quit it," she hisses, grabbing my arm. "I should have known you'd try to sabotage the night. What are you so afraid of—giving a shit?"

My skin flames, the heat rising from my feet to the crown of my head in one fell swoop. It's been a cruddy day on top of a crap-filled couple of years and I've had enough. I'm going home to grab the suitcase I never even had a chance to unpack, and then I'm getting the hell out of Dodge. It was a mistake to come back.

I lift my hands, palms out, and blink away tears of regret. "You were right earlier today—I don't belong. We can't even spend five minutes together without this... animosity between us. I'm going to hop on a bus to Berkeley. It's for the best."

I wrap quivering arms around her unresponsive

body, squeeze, and let go before she jerks free. "Tell Ben to call me anytime he needs to talk—you, too. And keep my car. It's not much, but it'll get you around, for a while, anyway. I'll send money for Mom's funeral and whatever you need, just let me know." I'm starting to crack, so I turn and blindly stumble into another set of arms—these ones strong and comforting.

"Come on," Simon murmurs. "I'll take you home."

I should argue, but instead, huddle into his side and allow him to lead me away. I'm weak, but for just a little longer I don't want to be alone. I have my whole life ahead of me for that honor.

Just before we walk out the door, I glance over his shoulder, but Izzy is gone and so are my hopes of a reconciliation.

CHAPTER THIRTEEN

IZZY

My elbow slips off the edge of the bar and I slosh my fourth—or is it fifth?—whiskey over my hand, the cold alcohol temporarily drawing me out of the dejected fog I've been sitting under for most of the night, ever since my sister left me standing on the dance floor.

In some soggy part of my muddled brain, I know it's my fault. I drove her away. "I'm a mess," I mumble, my head flopping onto my chest, too heavy for my neck.

"A train wreck, actually," a rumbling voice replies as a masculine hand moves the glass out of reach and gently wipes my fingers with a napkin.

I groan and try to stop the room from swirling. "Go 'way, Jay. Ha, I'm a poet and didn't even know it."

"You're many things, babe, but a poet isn't one of them. Why are you getting hammered sitting all alone in a bar?"

I want nothing more than to lean into the warmth of his arm wrapped around my back and let the night progress to its natural conclusion, but that isn't fair to Jay. He didn't sign up to babysit a drunk, and I still have enough common sense to know sex isn't the answer to this particular nightmare.

"Why did she have to come back?" I whine, and maybe even drool a little. "We don't need her, she's..."

"She's what, and who are you talking about?" Jay brushes lank strands of hair behind my ear and gazes at me quizzically.

"My sister. I don't want her here, Jay. Make her go 'way." I stare at him soulfully, then drop my head on his shoulder. "She going to break Benjamin's heart." *And mine.*

"I think you need to give her a chance, honey."

I jerk upright, knocking his jaw with my head. *Good.* He should be on my side anyway, *not hers.* "A chance to what, huh? Renée doesn't give a shit about us. She's only here to see what she can get out of Mom's will and then she'll put Smuggler's Cove in the rearview mirror for good."

"What can I get ya?" The bartender, a barrel-chested bull of a guy wandered down to our end of the bar and stood waiting, a stained cloth in one meaty paw.

I perk up and give him my best charming smile. "I'll have—"

"Thanks, we're good," Jay cuts in, sliding a twenty across the counter. "Be out of your hair soon."

The guy raises a brow but reaches under the counter and drops my keys on the bar. "Standard procedure. No Designated Driver, no keys."

I sink down, dejected at getting cut off while Jay nods and palms the keys to my beloved VW, Bessy. He waits for the man to amble away before taking my arm to help me off the scaffolding they call barstools in this place, which turns out to be a good thing as my legs have turned into the consistency of Mom's limp spaghetti noodles.

"Oops." I belch into the material pulled tautly over an outstanding set of pecs. I should know, I've been sleeping with the guy for months. Jay takes his health seriously and is consistently annoyed when I don't.

I pat his chest and gaze up at him with my best come-hither look, totally second-guessing my honorable intentions of a few minutes ago.

"Do you have something in your eye?" he asks,

squinting down at me like I'm some weird specimen on a slide.

Insulted, I push away and almost trip over the boots I spent half my paycheck on so I could feed the emptiness roaming like a caged lion in my breast. It didn't work.

"Give me my keys, Carlisle, I'm going home."

He gives me an indulgent smile and all but pats my head. "You know I can't do that. We'll leave your car here and stop by on the way to work in the morning to pick it up."

His warm arm enfolds me close again and I'm gently, but inexorably, ushered toward the doors, propped open to let the muggy stench of liquor and body heat escape. I try to hold onto my annoyance, but truthfully, I'm grateful Jay is here, I don't want to be alone with my thoughts.

"Hey, Izzy, is this guy bothering you?" Kyle appears out of nowhere, a concerned frown marring his smooth forehead.

I blink owlishly at him, Jay's arm suddenly feeling like the sword of Damocles on my shoulders. "N... no. K... Kyle, what are you doing here?" I pray my stutter either goes unnoticed or is attributed to the alcohol I'd consumed, and not the source of all my childhood fantasies standing in front of me.

He jerks his head toward the group of suits I'd

been eyeing when Renée and I first arrived and the guy I'd flirted with looks up—*crap*. I shudder and burrow deeper into Jay's armpit.

"I guess I didn't mention it before, but I flew in for the big conference in Seattle—technological innovation—and brought a few of my associates to see our Grizzly Mining Corporation." Kyle's eyes radiate excitement, and I stare at him bemused by this new and improved version of the boy I'd known. "There's been some groundbreaking advances in AI technology, as well as drones, smart sensors, automated digging... it can make a big difference to the environment and reduce production costs at the same time, a win-win." He grins at Jay with a flash of good ol' boy charm. "Didn't mean to step on your toes there, buddy, just watching out for my girl. We go back a long way, and I wouldn't want to see her get hurt." The warning comes couched in a smile, but the threat is there, nonetheless.

Before I could even think of a reaction to his overbearing attitude, Jay comes to my rescue. "It's none of my business, but if you're so worried about Izzy getting hurt, I would suggest you *invest* some time in getting to know the woman. She's smart, independent, sassy, and incredibly sexy. Furthermore, if you cared about her at all, you wouldn't let her sit alone in a bar knocking back drinks..." His arm drops to my waist and squeezes. "Now if you'll excuse us, we were just leaving."

"Oh, yeah, of course." Kyle steps aside to let us pass, his ears red. "I'll call you tomorrow, Izz."

"Ugh," I growl, twisting free the moment we're clear of the doors. "Are all men born Neanderthals?"

Jay chuckles, (chuckles!) until my expression warns him to quit while he's ahead. "Why, because we butted heads a bit? That's just posturing, babe. Guys are territorial by nature."

"Yeah, well I'm not looking to be captured, thank you very much." I stomp through the parking lot, weaving between a combination of new and vintage vehicles, fed up with life in general and men in particular.

"Slow down before you fall," Jay warns just as I trip over a boulder the size of Mt. Rushmore.

I stumble against the side of a car, swearing as my ankle turns in these damn boots I'll probably never wear again, then screech when my hand falls through the open passenger window.

"What the hell?" A woman shrieks back, shoving at my head and shoulders with talon-like hands digging into my skin.

Jay grabs me around the waist and drags me backward, my heart pumping out of my chest, and knocks my skull on the doorframe. "Ow!" I holler, not sure what hurts more, my ankle, my head, or my pride.

"Like I said, a walking disaster," Jay mutters in my ear, holding me upright against his chest.

"Whatever," I growl, rubbing my skull and trying to see through the dark to apologize to the person I'd inadvertently attacked. "I'm sor... ry." The words turn to dust on my tongue when I get my first clear look at the furious woman—Simon's fiancée, Lacey.

"You Thomas's can't keep your hands to yourself, can you?" She stares at me like I'm dirt under her high-priced shoe, haughty chin in the air.

"It was an accident, Lace," her cousin, Lisa, murmurs from the driver's seat.

"Whose side are you on?" Lacey shoots back, without taking her gaze from me. "Tell your sister to stay away from my fiancé, or she's going to be sorry."

I can't help it, I stiffen. It doesn't matter how pissed at Renée I am, she's family, and family sticks together. "Mess with her and you mess with me—leave my sister alone." I could have explained Renée will be gone before the leaves fall, but I'm not feeling generous. Let Lacey stew over her EMT stud muffin, not my problem.

"Why, you—"

The car door swings toward me and I tense for the upcoming confrontation, but Jay draws me backward, my heels dragging on the pavement.

"It's late and tempers are running high, let's take a

step away from this and address it with coffee tomorrow, on me." Jay huffs in a pained breath when I elbow him in the ribs. Why did he invite them to the café? Is he *trying* to drive me crazy?

"I'm taking a sick day, get someone to cover my shift." I stand next to his monster truck waiting for him to unlock the damn door so I can go home and drown my sorrows with the leftover box of wine in the fridge.

He opens the door and wraps his hands around my waist, lifting me up to the seat as though I weigh nothing. My pulse flutters, turned on whether I want to admit it or not. He knows it too, the creep.

He leans forward until our lips are a breath away, the heat of his body warming me from the inside out. "You, Izzy Thomas, are trouble with a capital T. Good thing I like a challenge," he mutters, his mouth taking mine in a soul-stealing kiss.

I moan and wrap my arms around his neck, my legs parting to let him in. "I'm mad at you," I mumble, nipping his bottom lip and getting a thrust of his hips in return. So good, but not enough. My hands slide down his arms braced against the doorjamb and tug at his shirt, trying without success to draw him closer. "Jay," I plead, desperate for physical contact.

Instead, he eases back, cupping my hands to his chest and looking at me with a mixture of searing passion and regret. It's the regret that bottoms out my stomach, not the alcohol I've consumed.

"I better get you home, it's late." He places a tender kiss on my knuckles then lets me go and closes the door, leaving me cold and alone.

But I should be used to that.

CHAPTER FOURTEEN

SIMON

The car is silent except for the muffled sniffles coming from the passenger seat. I glance over and reach for the heater—Renée is vibrating, huddled in the corner of the car with her hands covering her face.

"You need to calm down or you're going to make yourself sick, honey."

She hiccups rather endearingly, then spreads her fingers to stare at me with luminous eyes. "Wh... what did you say?"

I drag my gaze back to the road. "You need to calm... oh, that. Slip of the tongue, forget it." Calling her honey came naturally, after all, we were together for most of my high school years. At least until she walked away without an explanation.

"I'll have you home in a few minutes. You'll feel better after a good night's rest." And I'll be able to breathe again once she gets out of my car. The magnolia scent she'd always preferred is bringing back memories I can't afford to be having. It's not fair to Lacey, or me. Renée is my past and I want her to stay there. The sooner I get her out of my life, the better it will be.

"I can't go back there," she whispers half under her breath, then turns to me with a panicked expression. "Izzy hates me, Simon. I told her I would leave, and she seemed relieved. I can't go back there," she repeats.

I swerve a little at this surprising revelation and a driver in the oncoming lane warns me to pay attention with a sharp blast of the horn. I automatically straighten the car out, my mind buzzing with the reper-cussions of her confession. Who am I going to get to care for Grams on such short notice? She's scheduled to be released tomorrow and I've already put my name in for extra shifts at work to raise money for the wedding from hell. Lacey's parents covered her dress along with the bridesmaids, as well as the church and flowers—fresh, of course—but it's up to me to pay for the reception—at the golf club, no less—and our honey-moon to the Bahamas (Lacey's idea. I would have been happy with a tent and an intimate campsite in the woods). I can't take the time off, even if I wanted to, the captain is keeping the roster full until whoever is starting suspicious fires near schools is captured. And underlying all of this, is the churning in my gut at the thought of losing Renée again, just when I've found her.

"Stay with me," I blurt like a lovesick dolt. I'm not. I'm doing this for Grams and to help an old friend. Gracious under fire, that's me. "There's plenty of room in the loft. You can have my room and I'll take the couch. It's just for one night, after all. Grams will be home tomorrow, and you'll be moving in with her to keep to our agreement." As though reminding her of her obligation makes it honorable—*geez*.

I power down the window to get some air, wondering if my sweating brow and elevated heartbeat mean I'm about to have a stroke. It wouldn't surprise me. I don't know how guys who live double lives do it without keeling over from stress, and they're actively hiding the truth. I'm merely omitting a few facts in the interests of keeping the peace between me and my bride-to-be.

Yeah, right.

"I can go to a hotel. I don't want to cause any more hard feelings between you and your fiancée." She stares at me with miserable eyes, hands clasped in her lap. "I won't back out of my responsibility to your grandmother, if that's what you're worried about."

I swear and wheel into the nearest empty parking lot, a Mom and Pop grocery store closed for the night. Slamming the car into park, I sit for a moment staring out the front window trying to figure out how I got myself into this mess. The store's security lights spread a soft glow over the vehicle, in the distance, a car door closes startling a stray tabby scavenging near a dumpster at the end of the building. Normal sights and sounds on anything but a normal night.

"This isn't the way I pictured seeing you again," she murmurs, interrupting my quiet panic attack.

I turn my torso, resting my back against the door, and relish the cool air kissing my nape. "You thought about me while you were gone?" I shouldn't be so pleased by this unexpected confession, but I am. The first six months after she disappeared without a word gutted me, but then I became angry. Furious she thought so little of our relationship, not to mention her family's horrifying loss, that she couldn't even take the time to say goodbye. Or let us in on her suffering. I would have done anything for that girl. I'm not so sure about now.

"Of course." She nervously twirls a length of spun-gold hair, a gesture I'd seen her do a million times in the past. "It was hard for me, to be so far away, on my own."

"You're the one who left," I snap, the cool draft doing nothing to alleviate my rising blood pressure. "I wanted to help, Renée. To be there for you, but your sister said you packed up and left the same night your dad... Why? Your family needed you, honey." *I needed you.*

She flinches as though I hurt her when it's *my* heart that stings. "They were fighting that night, you know—my parents. It wasn't new, they were always arguing over something. Not enough money to pay the bills, Mom's burned dinners, Dad's dirty clothes all over the house, but this was different. Colder. Meaner."

She shivers again and I hurry to roll up the window rather than pull her over the console and into my empty arms.

"You didn't say anything when I picked you up for the party." I'm trying to understand, but the misery she's going through tangles with the bereft feelings I've carried for far too long, and the empathy I should be feeling—do feel— is coming out more like an accusation.

"What was I supposed to say, Simon? That our house had become a warzone? I didn't want my boyfriend to know our family was imploding and I didn't know how to fix it." She glares at me as if it's somehow my fault and strangely maybe it is. Was I so self-absorbed with football and senior year I didn't notice Renée was going through a stressful time?

"I wish you would have talked to me, let me in." I surprise us both by grasping her hand. "I'm sorry you lost your dad in such a horrible fashion, and now, with your mom..."

She stiffens and tugs her fingers free, the loss its own little death, and I curse my stupidity. "Don't worry, suicide isn't contagious. My mom died of quite normal causes, cancer to be precise." Snapping her seatbelt into place with a decisive click, she sits straight and stares out the window at the toilet paper tower taking up valuable real estate at the front of the store. "It's getting late, and I've had a long day. Take me to a hotel, Simon, it's for the best. I'll get a cab in the morning and be there when your grandmother comes home." She shoots me an inscrutable glance. "I keep *my* promises."

What is that supposed to mean? I open my mouth to argue, but one moment stretches to another, and then it's too late and I feel the loss as though she's already gone. Sighing, I nod and start the car but can't resist a parting comment. "I wonder where we would be today if you'd stuck around long enough to give me a chance. It must be lonely on that desert island you inhabit so no one can get into that place you call a heart."

Ignoring the aching void in my chest, I sedately drive to the nearest hotel, my words ringing hollowly in my ears.

CHAPTER FIFTEEN

RENÉE

After an endless day and sleepless night, I'm not in any shape to face my sister but know an apology is called for and should probably be made in person. The thought of a strong cup of coffee convinces me to quit procrastinating over my less-than-fresh appearance—I grimace at the wrinkled skirt and stained blouse smelling faintly of booze—and leave my hotel room for the short walk to The Voltage.

It's still early enough the heat promised in the robin's egg blue sky hasn't materialized yet, the air holding on to dawn's sweet tang. As songbirds twitter in the flowering plums lining the street, the mingling scents of magnolia, hyacinth, and lilac clear the cobwebs from my brain and allow me to smile for what feels like the first time since I crossed town limits. A garbage truck ambles past, stopping long enough for a worker to hop down and empty bins lined up like soldiers along the curb. It's been a long time since I could savor a quiet morning stroll. College was a series of lectures, studies, tests, rinse, repeat. More challenging than I'd expected. I ran away to forget and ended up finding a purpose—physical and psychological therapy, a way to make peace with my father's death.

There's a line of customers when I enter the café with Izzy at the front, directing the crowd with all the skill of a conductor. I hesitate, disappointed. It's not likely she's going to get a break any time soon, maybe I should have phoned first. Considering last night, it's probably for the best.

I turn for the door just as Izzy calls my name. I swing around, embarrassed as everyone turns their attention from cell phones to me.

She points to a table newly vacated in the corner and shrugs winningly at the man holding a folded newspaper in front of her. "Sorry, my sister." Lifting her chin, she meets my wary gaze. "Give me ten."

Nodding, I tuck my bag close to my body, edging around the clustered tables, and take a seat at the free one where I can watch Izzy in her element. For a Class A introvert like me, I find the aspect of dealing with hordes of consumers petrifying, but she handles them with consummate ease, sending one to the pick-up counter where a guy is frothing and mixing and steaming in front of an intimidating stainless-steel behemoth of a coffee machine. Another customer—a senior—is given a delectable-looking pastry and a numbered card, then gently directed to a table along the exposed brick wall that gives the room a warm, homey vibe.

It takes closer to twenty minutes to serve the morning rush, but finally, there's a lull, and after a couple of quick words with her coworker, who shoots me a glance from narrowed eyes and steepled brows, she grabs a couple of light blue cappuccino cups with matching saucers and makes her way across the room to dump them on the table in front of me.

"You look like you could use this," she says, gesturing at my clothes. "Is this your version of a walk of shame?"

"What?" I hiss, running another smoothing hand over my skirt. "Of course not. How can you say that?"

She shrugs and flops into the seat across from me, looking worn out. "It was a joke, okay? Not very funny, but then I'm not feeling very humorous at the moment, either. You ditched me last night. Left your barely legal sister in a bar full of sex-depraved men and women. How could *you* do that?"

Point taken.

I take a cautious sip of my drink and am pleasantly surprised by the burst of flavors. Deep, luscious coffee, frothy milk, vanilla, a hint of cinnamon, and nutmeg maybe? Whatever it is, it's addictive.

"Hardly sex-depraved, but I'm sorry. It was discourteous of me, but you were out to cause a fight and I wasn't up to it. Did you get home okay?"

Izzy uses her fingertip to draw an arrow through the creatively designed heart in her cup. "Jay showed up. He took care of me."

I glance at the counter and the handsome barista straightens, his gaze concerned as it rests on my sister. "How long have you two—?"

Izzy frowns and slouches in her seat. "It's none of your business who I screw, that's what you want to know, isn't it?"

"Isn't he kind of old for you?" I ignore her coarseness, knowing she's trying to get a rise out of me, but I'm genuinely concerned. I'd hate for her to be taken advantage of by a player.

"Jay's twenty-five, not sixty, for crying out loud. Mom and Dad were ten years apart—not that we're getting hitched or anything," she hurries to add, rolling her eyes. "We're friends, that's all. I'm more interested in you and Romeo. I notice you didn't come home last night." She waggles her brows and grins.

I'd forgotten her flashfire temperament, fighting mad one minute, laughing the next. "I assumed the locks would have been engaged and a chair under the doorknob." I'm only half kidding.

"You might be right, but that doesn't answer my question—did you spend the night with Simon Monroe or not?"

I flush guiltily. "He drove me to a hotel, Izz. End of story."

She chuckles. "Whatever you say, Rae-Rae." She glances at the growing lineup and sighs. "I need to get back to work. When do you leave?"

She still thinks I'm going, and for a moment, I'm tempted. I could be in Berkeley by nightfall, and resume my lonely existence, away from everyone and everything I love.

"I'm not going anywhere," I answer quietly, clearing my suddenly tight throat. "At least not yet. I promised I'd be there for you and Ben, and I meant it, little sister. You aren't getting rid of me that easily."

She freezes in the middle of rising from her chair and stares at me, hope and distrust warring in her expressive blue eyes. "You'll forgive me if I hold off on the celebration, I've needed you before and we all know how that went."

Ouch. I deserve her cynicism but can't deny it hurts.

"That's okay, baby sister, I'll wait." And I will. This time I'm not turning my back on my family.

———⟨◦⟩———

I'D BEEN TO SIMON'S GRANDMOTHER'S HOUSE A couple of times while we were dating and remember it as an elegant but comfortable craftsman bungalow, different in every way from our mid-century rancher hodge-podged together with various additions over the years.

I stare up the cobblestone driveway to the white house with black shutters and colorful flowerboxes nestled amid a stand of giant fir trees like a fairytale cottage. I'd foolishly dreamed this house could someday be ours, mine, and Simon's. Until the night he betrayed our love and my father committed suicide, proving what I'd already known, trusting anyone is a mistake.

The driveway gently slopes upward and is lined with rhododendrons in shades of pink and daylilies with long green knife-edged fronds. Butterflies take flight in my stomach at the sight of Simon's Barracuda parked off to the side, in front of a two-story wood and stone building. A single-car garage with barn doors is on the bottom, but it's the double-paned dormer window reflecting light above that draws my eye. Is he still in bed, spreadeagled and naked except for a pair of tight-fitting boxers over drool-worthy glutes with arms cradling his pillow, highlighting smooth and muscular lats? Or maybe he's in the shower, soap covering his chest and arrowing lower...

Is he even alone?

"Are you going to stand there all day, or join me for breakfast? I'm not getting any younger, you know."

A girly squeal bursts from my lungs as I swing around, hands fluttering wildly in the air. "Mrs. O'Brian! I didn't see you there."

She gives me a knowing look and turns her walker toward a pumpkin orange front door. "I'm not surprised. You were a bit preoccupied. Come on now, Simon will be down in a while."

Cheeks hot, I hurry to catch up, though I'm beginning to wonder what I'm doing here. She seems to be getting around just fine, and her acerbic tongue hasn't suffered from the accident, either.

"I wasn't looking for your grandson," I deny, avoiding her eyes as I reach around to open the door for her. "When were you released? I thought I'd be here in ample time for your arrival."

She shuffles awkwardly into the house and lumbers down a narrow hallway covered in family photos to a bright and cheery kitchen painted buttery yellow with white cupboards and trim. The mouthwatering scent of maple bacon draws me nose first into the room and over to a table laden with a smorgasbord of muffins, pancakes, strawberries, orange slices, English muffins, and pints of homemade jam.

Mrs. O'Brian slumps into a chair and waves to a burbling coffee machine on the counter. "Would you mind, dear? I wanted to have everything ready when Simon finishes his shower but I'm not up to snuff quite yet."

Shower, then. The flush that had just started to cool from my cheeks explodes in my torso, trailing from breast to stomach and lower. Simon introduced me to the sensual pleasures of making love in a steamy shower—an intimate world for two. I know the sage and sandalwood scent of his soap, the groans of passion when we kissed, his trembling when I dropped to my knees and took his...

I jerk, spilling hot coffee over the rim of the cup I'm holding and onto my hand. I set the mug down before I drop it and suck on the reddened skin between my thumb and forefinger. "Dammit," I mutter, as much for the burn as my erotic thoughts.

"Dear? Is everything all right?" Mrs. O'Brian stares at me with a furrowed brow, probably wondering what she'd let herself in for. She's not the only one.

"Yes, sorry, I'm such a klutz." This time I focus on

what I'm doing and make it to the table without mishap. Setting a cup within reach of Mrs. O'Brian, I take a seat and try not to worry about Simon's imminent appearance. "How are you feeling? Did the doctor give you a list of exercises to do? Medication? I want to set up a daily regimen as soon as possible. The longer we hold off, the stiffer we'll get."

"First," she says, breaking a blueberry muffin in half and slathering butter on each side with a liberal hand. "There is no *we*. You are a healthy, beautiful young lady while I am... not. Reginald—Dr. Dunsmuir," she glances up and points the muffin in my direction before taking a delicate nibble from the side, "released me into your tender care and I'm sure you will have me back to normal in no time at all, but for now... Oh, there you are, my boy. Just in time, we were about to start without you."

I freeze, a strawberry halfway to my lips as Simon strolls over to the coffee pot, the tantalizingly fresh scent of soap and man taking my breath away. He's in uniform, the navy-blue pants hugging hips and thighs before flaring slightly down to shiny black work shoes. His chestnut hair is still damp and curls on his nape. I clench my hand in my lap, recalling the way it used to wrap around my fingers as though binding me to him, two souls as one.

"You came," he says, lifting a steaming cup of

coffee to his mouth and blowing gently before taking a sip.

And I'd been fantasizing about the jerk? I deliberately suck the end of the strawberry between my lips and take a slow, succulent bite before arching a delicate brow. "I said I would. We were just about to go over her physiotherapy plan, so if you need to leave..."

Eyes fixated on my mouth, Simon swallows too much coffee and chokes. He shoots me a glare and turns to the sink, harsh coughs erupting from his chest.

Mrs. O'Brian chuckles. "You two sound like me and the Mister. when we first met. No one knew whether we were foes or friends. Turns out opposites attract—who knew?"

"You and Pops had something special, Grams, a one-in-a-million relationship." He washes his hands, then joins us at the table to give his grandmother a hug and kiss on the cheek. "Pops always swore he won the lottery the day you said yes to his marriage proposal."

She pats his arm, a light flush suggesting a youthful beauty. "That man was such a charmer, how could I say no? You're just like him, don't you agree, Renée dear?"

Simon smirks as he takes a seat across from me and reaches for the bacon. "Leave her be, Grams. We don't want to scare her away on the first day. How are you feeling? You should be resting, not creating a buffet for twenty lumberjacks."

Is that a stab at me? "I would have been here sooner if *someone* had informed me of your grandmother's release time."

He tosses a couple of rashers of bacon on my plate and adds a serving spoon of scrambled eggs on the side before filling his dish. "Talk to Grams about that. She bribed Doc Dunsmuir to bring her home. I only found out myself when I called the hospital and found she'd already left. Grams?"

She shrugs good-naturedly. "I'm old enough to make my own decisions, young man. And if I want to cook my grandson and his friend a light breakfast, I will. Now eat, before it gets cold."

"Yes, ma'am," Simon and I say in unison, sharing a secretive smile before dropping our gazes to our plates.

I have the impression Mrs. O'Brian is matchmaking. What I don't understand is why. Simon's engaged. He's not mine for the taking even if it were a possibility, which it isn't. I poke at my airy scrambled eggs, appetite gone. I thought reuniting with my sister was going to be tough, but the feelings lurking in my chest for the man currently spreading marmalade on toast for his grandmother threatens everything I've worked to overcome—and scares me to death.

CHAPTER SIXTEEN

IZZY

I sigh when the last of the lunch crowd vacates the coffee shop leaving blessed silence in their wake, other than piped-in music from Jay's favorite singer, Billie Eilish. It's been a hellish day and it isn't over yet —I still have a meeting at the school over Benjamin's truancy and an entire brass band has taken up residence behind my temples.

Finished with clearing tables and wiping them down, I stop by the office to let Jay know I'm leaving. He's hunched over, pecking at the keyboard, an intense frown marring his brow, the store's accounts on the computer screen.

"Problems?" I lean against the doorframe. Jay's always done his bookkeeping, and since the café seems busy, I've never given a thought to the added pressure he must be under to keep things running smoothly. Considering my financial situation and the juggling I have to do each month to make ends meet, it's a miracle he does so well.

"Hmm?" He glances up, expression vague. Then his gaze sharpens, and he drops the lid on the laptop with all the casualness of a rocket launcher. "Nah, just catching up before month end." He taps the desk, inviting me over. "Are you ready for the big meeting?"

As a diversion, it's good, but not enough to quell the hard lump forming in my gut. If the coffee shop is in trouble, so am I. I've worked here for three years, it's all I know. If I need to find another job now, it's bound to affect my application process to get legal guardianship of Benjamin.

I wander into the room and perch on the edge of the desk between his spread legs. At this level, we're eye-to-eye and the stress and weariness on his craggy face are more apparent. He puts in double the hours I work, does community events, and volunteers at a homeless shelter downtown without complaint. Suddenly, my whining feels churlish and even worse, childish.

"Why do you put up with me?" I cup his face and gaze into the warm brown-sugar depths of his eyes, the bristles already forming since his morning shave tickling my palms.

His gaze softens, stirring the embers of lust that are never very far away in our interactions. "I could ask the same of you." He leans forward and our lips meld as though they're two halves of a whole. When he sits back, I'm breathing faster, and my nipples are hard. "We're good together, Izz. We understand each other."

Yeah, we do. No strings attached, friends-with-benefits, work buddies, that's us. The millennial relationship dynamic duo. Except, what if I want more? Is there something wrong with the Thomas women? Mom couldn't save Dad, Renée lost Simon, and I've ruined every fling I've had since puberty. Maybe we aren't *forever after* type gals.

"I can almost hear the wheels turning in that complex brain of yours. What's wrong?" Jay tips his head in the way he has of investing a hundred percent in what I'm thinking, as though my ideas matter. I gotta admit, it's good for my flagging ego.

"Do you ever think of taking this... thing further?" I wave my hands back and forth between our bodies, already embarrassed I brought it up. "Not married or anything," I hasten to add. "Just, you know, the next step." Flustered, I sit back and stare at his chin. Why did I open my big mouth? *Less is more*, Dad preached often enough. You'd think I'd have it ingrained in my skull by now.

He grasps my hands and squeezes, forcing me to meet his surprised/shocked? gaze and my heart plummets to my toes. "Never mind, it was a stupid idea. Call it spring fever, or something." I attempt to rise and get the hell out before I say anything else, but Jay doesn't let me go. He tightens his grip on my wrists and tenses, enclosing my thighs in the band of his legs.

"Not so fast. You caught me off-guard but that doesn't mean it's a dumb idea. Only... you're young, Izzy. You have your whole life in front of you. Hell, in a few years, when Ben is old enough, you should travel, see the world, experience *life*." He tugs on my hands, draws me down onto his lap, and kisses my forehead. "You're free now, honey. I don't want you to make a decision you'll only regret later."

Free. I'd laugh but I'm afraid I might not be able to stop. Freedom is for those without responsibilities. I haven't been unrestricted since I was in diapers. I've gotten the message though. Jay isn't interested in anything more than a casual hookup now and then, at least not with me. But, I don't think I'm that girl anymore.

Forcing a carefree smile, I tap the end of his nose with my finger. "You better let me up before a customer finds us back here fraternizing. You don't want to wreck your studly image now, do you?"

I slide off his lap, heading for the door and my escape. "Besides, if I don't get moving, I'll be late for the meeting, and I don't want to give Mrs. Bains any more ammunition. Benjamin is in enough trouble already."

"Wait," Jay calls, rising to his formidable six-foot-five height. "Are we good?"

A lump forms in my chest the size of a basketball. Maybe it's losing Mom or reuniting with my sister, but I've changed. I can't be what he needs any more, and the loss is killing me.

"No," I say, tears tumbling down my cheeks. "I don't think we are."

———⟨๑⟩———

AN HOUR LATER I'M DIRECTED BY A SECRETARY into the school guidance counselor's office, but halt abruptly in the doorway when I see Mrs. Bain is not alone. Seated in one of the two mismatched visitor chairs is the blonde I saw Kyle with at Voltage the other day. *What is she doing here?*

"I'm sorry, am I early?"

Mrs. Bain rises, straightening her crisp white

blouse tucked into a black skirt. "No, no you're right on time." She gestures to the still-seated woman. "Miss Thomas, may I present Tabitha Webster. She is the court-appointed liaison in your case. It's her job to make sure Benjamin is placed in a home where he will thrive. She's here today to explain the procedure and answer any questions you may have. Please have a seat and we'll get started."

Hands sweaty, I slide into the other chair, stifling the resentment simmering in my stomach. It's just like the court to spring this on me with no warning. Tabitha Webster—Kyle's Tabitha—is wearing another of her power suits, lustrous hair twisted into one of those fancy buns that look casual but probably took an hour to create. Shiny black stilettos with blood-red soles show off slim ankles and shapely legs curled to the side all ladylike. I hate her on principle. She's everything I'm not and she holds my family's future in pink-tipped fingers.

"Miss Thomas, I'm sorry for your recent loss. I know it must seem overwhelming, but that's why I'm here. We all want what's best for your brother." Tabitha gazes at me with empathy radiating from serious green eyes, inviting me to trust this stranger, but I'm not biting.

"*I'm* what's best for my brother. We were doing fine until you people interfered, and now Benjamin is acting out because he's scared he's going to be taken away. Can you promise that's not going to happen, Miss Webster?" I clench my hands, more afraid than I've been since Renée left town. Ben is all I have left. I can't lose him.

"Miss Thomas—Izzy—no one is taking your brother from his home. At least not yet," Mrs. Bains assures me, glancing at the court liaison for agreement.

Tabitha smiles but refrains from either agreeing or contradicting the counselor. Instead, she lifts a leather satchel from where it rests against the leg of her chair and withdraws a sheaf of legal-looking documents, which she hands to me. "This is a simple agreement between the court and the child's temporary guardian—"

"Permanent," I insert, clenching the papers in nerveless fingers. "I'm Benjamin's permanent guardian. My mother wanted it that way."

"I understand." Tabitha nods. "Did she leave a living will stating her wishes? I believe your father... died a few years ago and your mother became sick not long after, is that correct?"

"Miss Webster, is this necessary?" Mrs. Bains stares at Tabitha with pinched lips and a furrowed brow.

Pain, old and new, lances my chest. It's the same whenever someone mentions my dad and his suicide, the awkward hesitation and false sympathy, the morbid curiosity they'd never admit to.

"Yes, my father killed himself if that's what you're asking. Don't worry, it's not contagious," I say, smirking as she leans away as though avoiding my airspace. "Mom developed lung cancer a few months later and refused treatment—she'd lost her will to live. And no, there are no documents pertaining to Benjamin's care, we didn't see the need. After all, he has two sisters, he's not alone."

"I wasn't aware there was anyone else in the picture." Tabitha makes a note in her cell phone, then looks up enquiringly. "Will she be a co-guardian moving forward?"

My stomach knots, why did I mention Renée? What am I supposed to say now? Sorry, my sister doesn't handle responsibility well.

"Look, I realize I'm barely over the legal age and don't have a fancy career, but I've held the same job for three years—" Which may be coming to an end if Jay can't get the business in the black again. "Cared for my mom throughout her illness, and managed household expenses along with my brother's school and sports activities. I know what I'm doing."

"We're not questioning your dedication, Miss Thomas. Benjamin is a well-rounded student thanks in large part to your influence." Mrs. Bains gives me a pacifying smile. "I think our main concern is for you—"

"I don't—"

"You've sacrificed much of your teenage years for your family," Mrs. Bains speaks over my interruption, determined to make her point. "But truthfully, you *are* a young, single woman and Benjamin is a growing boy. What happens if you meet someone who wants your attention? How will you fit your brother into such a scenario?"

I could state I've managed that *scenario,* as she put it, just fine for the last year and a half, but confessing I'm sleeping with my boss probably isn't in my best interests.

Crossing my arms, I meet her gaze square on, aware I'm fighting for the future of our family here. "Ben is more than my brother, Mrs. Bains. He's the last remaining link I have with my mom and dad. He's the best of all of us and I would do anything for him. *Anything,*" I repeat, tears hovering.

"Please understand, we don't mean to make you feel as though you're under attack." Tabitha cuts in, leaning forward with a tissue. "I know this is hard, but, like you, we have Benjamin's best interests at heart and only want to help you through this trying time. Why don't you take those papers home, read them over, and we could meet again, say in a month? I believe you have your mother's funeral to organize, that's more than enough to contend with at the moment."

Relieved to have this stay of execution, I nod gratefully and rise, shoving the documents into my canvas backpack. "Thanks, the service is Monday. I'd like to keep Ben home another week if that's okay?"

Mrs. Bains's empathetic gaze is hard to meet. "I'm so sorry you have to handle this on your own. If there's anything you need..."

Embarrassed, I shake my head and turn for the door. "We're fine, but thanks. I'll have Benjamin back in class in a week, then."

"I hope so, Miss Thomas. I hope so."

The warning implicit in her words follows me down the hall and out the door, its weight an anvil on my shoulders.

CHAPTER SEVENTEEN

SIMON

I gather up the last of our medical supplies and return them to the go-bag while Dobbs finishes up with the patient. We've been answering call after call ever since our shift began; two overdoses, a senior with a broken leg, a beloved cat up a tree—who wasn't grateful for our intervention—and then this, a teen with a cutting fetish that almost cost her life.

The parents hover by the girl's bedside, pale and teary-eyed—dazed. The walls are papered in unicorns and rainbows, the bed is a white canopy with eyelet ruffle covers. Everything is a stark contrast to the patient with dyed ink-black hair, multiple earrings in one ear, and a flesh tunnel in the other big enough to put a quarter through. Her arms are marked with thin red lines, the right wrist swaddled in gauze and tape. She keeps her head turned away, staring at the flowering dogwood out her window possibly, or maybe nothing at all.

I hate these calls. Even though we've saved her life —this time—I feel helpless. How long before we need to return, maybe too late the next time? She needs help, this girl who cuts herself like silent screams of some internal trauma I can't even imagine. Though I barely know her, I want to slay her dragons, but I don't know where to start.

"Nicole, talk to us, please." Her mother sobs, hand out as though to brush her daughter's hair, but afraid to touch her in case she breaks.

"Honey, stop, you'll make yourself ill. If Nicky wants to act like a petulant child, she can. She'll have plenty of time to think over her actions while she's grounded—for the next year, at least." Nicole's father tightens his protective hold on his wife and glances at Dobbs and then me. "Thank you for coming, you can see yourselves out."

Irritated, though it's not my concern, I give a brisk nod but ignore him to move to the opposite side of the bed and crouch where Nicole lies still as death. I slip a card from my palm and tuck it under the edge of her pillow on the pretense of straightening the covers. Her empty, sedative-induced gaze meets mine before the blue-veined lids close, shutting me out. The world out.

"We're only a phone call away if you need us," I tell her, trying to impress the fact she matters—we care. She responds by turning her head away.

"If you're through, my family would like some privacy." The father glowers, practically kicking us out the door.

I rise slowly, staring him down over his daughter's inert body. "We've done the best we can for Nicole, but she should come with us. A day or two in the hospital will ensure her recovery goes smoothly." I don't mention the suicide watch protocol that would no doubt be put in place.

His wife covers her mouth and sways, possibly grasping the seriousness of the situation. "Tony, maybe..."

"No," he snaps, making his wife and daughter jump. "I take care of my own. Nicole will *never* do this again because she knows the consequences. Now, please, if you'll excuse me," his smile is more a baring of teeth, "I'd like to spend this enforced day home from work watching over my girl with my wife." He yanks her closer, digging his fingers into her shoulder.

Dobbs gives me a warning look, closing his clipboard and picking up the discarded go-bag. "Sure thing. If you have any problems—"

"We'll call. Thank you, gentlemen, we're fine." The father turns his back on us, blocking any further views of Nicole.

Left with no alternative, I follow Dobbs into the hall, easing the door shut. There was no time earlier, but now it's impossible to miss the elegant tables, Persian runners, or expensive paintings decorating the walls. Too bad all this ostentatious wealth couldn't protect his girl from the monsters driving her to self-injure.

"Can you believe that guy?" I slam the side panel on the ambulance and hop into the passenger seat, frustration making me short-tempered. "He's more concerned with appearances than his daughter's well-being. There should be something we can do."

Dobbs locks in his seatbelt and starts the van before sliding me a glance. "Well, there isn't, not unless it happens again. Look, we have a file started. The health authority will read it and probably follow up with a wellness check. We did our job, that's all we can do."

I sit back, his words reverberating in my head, as he shifts into gear and bumps down the uneven pavement to the road. Sometimes, all we can do isn't enough.

———⟨∘⟩———

It's after midnight by the time our shift ends, and I'm beat. I briefly consider catching a few hours of rest at the station, but the lure of my bed pulls me home. It's got nothing to do with a certain blonde staying in my grandmother's house—or so I tell myself.

The streets are quiet. It's the beginning of June, but already summer heats the air. Skeletal fingers of fog create halos around the lampposts and drift through the treetops invoking thoughts of the upcoming fair. I've booked the weekend off so I can take Lacey on the rides and attend the bachelor party I'm not supposed to know anything about. A night I'm not looking forward to. Excessive alcohol, and knowing the guys, strippers, doesn't hold the appeal it once might have. The wedding is creeping up, a lot like this fog, and so is the feeling of entrapment. Does every groom have misgivings?

Lacey is great. She's beautiful, funny, popular, and wants the same things I want, the white picket fence fantasy along with a house full of kids. I enjoy spending time with her, and we have a good sex life. She's creative and generous in bed. Hell, am I reading a profile on a dating website or thinking about my soon-to-be wife? I love Lacey, I'm not as sure if I'm *in* love with her—and that's a problem.

Grams left the porch light on for me, a welcoming glow in the dark. I'd missed that symbol of her affection while she was in the hospital. It's opened my eyes to how precious she is to me and how uncertain life can be. I vow to cherish the time we have together and never take her for granted again.

Leaving the 'Cuda at the end of the drive since it's late and the road runs close to the house, I stop to breathe in the night air and release some of the tension I've carried since leaving young Nicole in the questionable care of her parents. If it was up to me, she'd be in a hospital bed right now under the watchful eyes of nurses and a competent doctor who would encourage her to seek counseling, but my hands are tied.

"You seem deep in thought."

My heart pole-jumps into my throat, which is good as it prevents the girlish shriek from escaping my lips. "Are you *trying* to give me a heart attack?"

I search the shadows near the house until I spot Renée sitting on the swinging loveseat I built Grams for her seventieth birthday. "What are you doing up so late?" Now my guts have joined the party, flittering and fluttering as though I've swallowed a field of fireflies.

"Waiting for you," she admits, setting the bench

rocking. "I need to talk to you about your grandmother."

Fear pushes everything else aside and I take the stairs two at a time heading for the door.

"Wait, Simon, it's not what you think." Renée leans forward, hand outstretched to stop me. "She's sleeping. Don't go rushing in there and wake her up, it took a while for her to settle."

I hesitate, but the relaxed way she's rocking the swing in pink pajama tops and bottoms with fuzzy white slippers convinces me it's not the emergency I'd pictured in my head, so I lean on the railing and take stock of my ex. Her hair is bundled into some kind of messy knot on top of her head, strands sticking out here and there as though refusing to conform to restraints—like the woman. Now that I'm not freaking out, I notice the white sheep frolicking on her cotton PJs and the black one grazing on her breast—lucky sheep.

Jerking my eyes up, I find Renée's gaze wandering my torso in a slow appraisal that stirs the attraction I've been working to quell. I need Grams to get better soon so our lives can go back to normal, minus Renée.

I straighten and clear my throat. "So, umm, how did she make out today? Much pain?" I'd called a couple of times through the afternoon, but she'd been resting which is to be expected after the injury she'd sustained.

"A bit. We did a few low-impact exercises to limber up the big muscle groups. I didn't want to push her too much until the soft tissue damage has time to heal. She has large contusions near the L4 vertebra along with shooting pains from her lower back to her toes that worries me. If it's not better tomorrow, I'll call Dr. Bains to get his opinion." She quits rocking and toes off her slippers to sit cross-legged on the bench, reminding me unbearably of the teenager I fell so hard for in high school.

"Maybe I should check in on her before bed," I say, then curse my fertile mind, though Renée isn't making it easy on me. Her toenails, painted an interesting tangerine orange, peek from under her legs, a contrast to the cotton candy pajama bottoms hugging her thighs, and the V-neck button-down top dipping between obviously unfettered breasts. Not that I'm looking.

"You can, of course, but she won't thank you for it. I offered to sit with her until she fell asleep, and do you know what she said?"

"I'm old enough to put myself to bed," I answer, a smile curving my lips. "Grams has always been independent, it drove Pops nuts."

Renée plays with the hem of her shirt, a pensive look on her pretty face. "You're lucky, I never knew my grandparents."

Though I shouldn't, I lower myself next to her, setting the bench gently rocking. "I've been meaning to say how sorry I am for the loss of your mom. She was a nice lady." I grimace at the inane comment. I won't be writing for any greeting card companies with benign lines like that.

Moved to try again, I place a hand on her knee. "What I meant to say is your mom always had time for your friends. She made us feel welcome in her home, and even fed us on more than one occasion—she was cool."

Renée nods, and a few more strands of silky hair escape their coil to drift lovingly against her nape. "She *was* cool. Dad..." She stops for a moment, and I grasp her hand, empathy tightening my throat. "Dad worked long hours and Mom was lonely, I think. It made her happy when we brought people home. It brought laughter to what was often an empty house."

We sit there for a few minutes, lost in thoughts of the past, then she gently squeezes my fingers and rises. "I better get in there, in case she needs me."

I'm bereft, as though she's about to walk out of my life for the second time and I have to bite back the protest choking my throat. "Of course, it's late. I have an early shift tomorrow, but if you need me—for anything—call."

I hurry to open the door, then stand aside to let her

pass, the flowery scent of her shampoo filling my head with memories I need to bury deep. "Goodnight, Renée."

She peeks up at me from under moon-dipped lashes. "Thank you, Simon, good night." And then she is through the door and gone, leaving me standing on the outside—again.

CHAPTER EIGHTEEN

RENÉE

I didn't expect to get any rest after my conversation with Simon last night, but I slept like a baby. We've always shared a deep connection, right from the first day we met when I was a freshman, and he took pity on the new kid by taking me under his wing until I found my feet. I've never forgotten his kindness to me —a scrawny, bookish introvert. After watching him over our time together, and now with his grandmother, I know it's an integral part of his personality.

I have many regrets from the night I ran away. My older, wiser self wishes I could whisper caution to my younger self and slow down to consider the conse-quences of my decisions. Like leaving my family when they needed me the most, and walking away from

Simon without confronting him over his betrayal. Even though there are still feelings between us, I need to step back and allow Simon to marry the girl of his choice—no matter how much it hurts.

I can't erase the past, but I can make reparations.

"Just five more, Mrs. O'Brian, you're doing so well." I keep a careful eye on my patient's discomfort level while bracing the walker she's using for balance as she gingerly stands, then gratefully lowers her weight on one of the straight-backed kitchen chairs.

"You said that five repetitions ago, young lady. I never took you for a slavedriver." She grimaces, but draws herself up again, arms quivering.

This is where the caregiver in me wants to take over, end the exercises and make Mrs. O'Brian a hot cup of tea, but it wouldn't be doing her a favor. The longer it takes her to get upwardly mobile, the more risk there is for permanent soft tissue damage. Already today, I notice stiffness in her movements compared to yesterday morning when she was fresh from the hospital, and the intravenous pain medications she'd received under Doctor Dunsmuir's care.

"I have complete faith in you—last one." I breathe a relieved sigh and smile as Mrs. O'Brian sinks onto the chair with a triumphant whoosh of air.

"Well, that was harder than I expected." Voice shaky, she pulls a tissue from a nearby box, pats her forehead and blows her nose, fingers trembling. "I must be getting old."

I pat her arm in commiseration, then move to make that tea and give her time to regain her composure. "You've been through a traumatic accident. It will take time for your body to heal."

"I don't know what happened. I was worried about running late for a lunch date and recall looking at my wristwatch. Next thing I know, I'm lying on the ground with a crowd of strangers leaning over me." She rubs her wristband and stares at the clockface as though it can scale back time.

My stomach rolls, her words horrifying me all over again. "Mrs. O'Brian, I don't know what to say. My mind was on other things, and I guess I wasn't paying as much attention as I should have been." The kettle starts whistling, giving me time to gather myself while I make our tea and add a couple of delicious-looking oatmeal raisin cookies to the tray.

I carry the laden tray to the table and carefully set a delicate cup and saucer of steaming green tea in front of her along with pots of milk and sweetener nearby. "My heart nearly stopped when I saw your head over the hood of Mabel..."

"You named your vehicle?" Mrs. O'Brian hesitates with her spoon over the sugar bowl, giving me a quizzical smile.

"I did," I admit with a sheepish grin. "Mabel may not be fancy, but she's reliable." After breaking a cookie in half and dunking the end into my cup, I sigh. "It's nice of you to let me work off my guilt this way. I couldn't believe I hit you like that, and then, Simon—"

"Ah, Simon." Mrs. O'Brian leans back, holding her cup to her chest. "My grandson is a handsome man, don't you think?"

My cheeks an embarrassing apple-red, I concentrate on doctoring my tea rather than meet the knowing glint in her match-making eyes. "I haven't noticed."

She chuckles. "If you say so. I seem to remember you were fairly smitten not all that many years ago. Forgive an old woman, but what happened to you two? I've never seen Simon as carefree and happy as he was with you."

I freeze, my heart thumping. "He's getting married, Mrs. O'Brian. Whatever we had, it's over. He's moved on... and so have I." *Or at least, I'm trying.*

She vehemently shakes her head, sloshing a bit of tea onto her peach blouse. "Lacey is a nice enough girl, but she's not the one for my grandson. He needs someone as strong as he is. Someone he can be himself with. Someone like you."

It's wrong how much I want that, too. But even if Simon were free, I'd still avoid a relationship—I'm broken. Everything I knew of love and security died with my dad.

"I'm sorry, Mrs. Bains, but I'm only here for the summer. My mom passed away a few days ago. I need to make sure my younger sister and brother are going to be okay, then I'm going back to a good job in California. My life is there now."

"Katherine, please. I believe we know one another well enough for first names. I'm very sorry for your loss. If there's anything Simon or I can do to help..."

"Thanks, but I think Izzy has most of the arrangements in hand. It's Benjamin I worry about. He's only twelve and has lost both parents. It's bound to affect him for years to come."

She stretches across the table and grasps my hand, compassion turning her faded blue eyes denim soft. "I'm sure it's hard on all of you. You're a good girl, Renée. Don't forget to take care of yourself while you're helping all of us."

I smile and blink back tears, breaking our connection to reach for my cup. It's been years since anyone showed concern for me, and the feeling is overwhelming. For just a moment I close my eyes and imagine a different scenario, one where my family is alive and well, and Simon never betrayed me and broke my heart.

Too bad dreams are for fools.

CHAPTER NINETEEN

IZZY

The day of the funeral dawns bleak, with turgid gray clouds obliterating the sunrise and shedding tears on the horizon. Shivering from a combination of nerves and the chilly morning air, I turn up the thermostat, then just as quickly turn it down, dollar signs rolling up through the heat vents.

Rubbing my aching temples, I double up on the pain meds and swallow them down with lukewarm water. Sighing, I wrap a sweater over my onesie pajamas and sink into a chair at the kitchen table. The eulogy I've spent hours on stares me in the face, mocking the brevity of the words. It reads like a generic bio written by a stranger. Is this the best I can do for the woman who gave me life? The mother who made sure food was on the table, clean clothes on our backs, and a roof over our heads? The wife who tried her damnedest to hold her family together with an increasingly morose, and often drunk, husband? Mom may have given up on her life but she never gave up on us. The least I can do is give her a proper send-off.

The pen is scratchy on the paper, scraping already frayed nerves. Tossing it aside, I reach for Benjamin's school bag shoved against the wall, and grunt at the weight. No wonder kids walk around with hunched shoulders, they pack anvils on their backs. When tugging doesn't work, I use the yank and twist method to break his binders free of the bag, stack them to the side, then delve to the bottom of the pack in search of a new pen. Instead, I find a crumpled piece of drawing paper. Something about it prickles my spine.

Feeling furtive in my own house, I rise, cringing when my chair screeches on the beat-up linoleum, and peek around the corner, my heart clip-clopping like a runaway train. Ben's bedroom door is closed, the hallway dark and silent.

Easing back to my chair, I spread the paper out with both hands and suck in a harsh breath at the detailed drawing revealed. "Oh, Benjamin, what have you done?"

Violent flames shoot into an innocent blue sky, sending plumes of black smoke billowing over a single-story cinder block building, a deserted children's playground with climbing bars, and a trio of swings in the background. One swing is off-kilter, the chain longer on one side than the other. It strikes at my heart, the lonely, broken piece of equipment that seems to have no place among the rest. Is Benjamin having trouble at school? And what does this fire signify?

I carefully fold the paper and tuck it into my pocket, then hurry to replace his books before he comes out and accuses me of going through his things. It's times like this I wish Mom was still here, even if she didn't have anything to say, which was the case more often than not the last few months before she died. I could try Jay but I'm off work for a few days to handle the funeral and avoiding him seems like a good idea after our blowout on Saturday. That leaves Renée. My gut cramps just thinking of admitting I may have failed our little brother when he needed me most. Maybe I should just ask him about it. He could be working on an art project, or something equally benign, and I'm making a big deal out of nothing.

A glance at the time blinking at me from the microwave confirms that it will have to wait until later —the funeral is only a couple of hours away and I need to get moving. Today will be hard. Mom was the glue that held our family together. I don't know where we'll go after this, and it scares me.

My phone chirps a text message, then another and another, filling me with panic. What now? I pull the cell phone out of my pocket—the crinkled paper burning the back of my fingers—to see it's from Renée.

Ready for today?

How am I supposed to answer that? Of course, I'm not ready. Who is ever ready to bury a parent? And we've had the misfortune of saying goodbye to our father and now, our mother.

I guess. You?

Look at us having a decent conversation. Maybe there's hope for us yet.

Mrs. O'Brian would like to attend. Simon is going to drive us. Do you and Benjamin need a lift?

SHE'S BEEN IN TOWN A WEEK AND ALREADY inserted herself into Simon's life. Figures, my world is in a downward spiral, and hers...

Nah, we'll walk. We can use the fresh air before making nice to the Sympathetic Widow's Club.

???

I SMIRK, KNOWING MY IRREVERENCE WILL exasperate her.

The seniors—mostly widows—who go from funeral to funeral dispersing sympathy to enjoy the comradery and free lunches.

Izzy, that's a horrible thing to say!

I SHRUG. SOMETIMES, THE TRUTH HURTS. I'M tempted to mention Simon's fiancée, but that truth will bring up hard feelings and I'm not up to the conflict today.

See you there. I'll save you a seat.

THREE DOTS APPEAR AND I WAIT FOR THE GENTLE rebuke, but then it disappears and the screen goes silent.

Sighing, I set the phone on the table and trudge down the hall to Ben's room. "Hey, buddy, time to get up. It's a busy day and I need you awake and prepared, okay? By the way, I had your suit dry-cleaned. It's hanging in your closet."

I tap my knuckles on the door and wait for a moan, groan, pillow against the wall. Anything telling me he's coherent, but the room stays quiet. Too quiet.

Edging the door open, I peer into the dimness, then swear low and long. Benjamin's bed has not been slept in. My twelve-year-old brother never came home last night, and I have no idea where he could be.

CHAPTER TWENTY

SIMON

The cards shuffle smoothly between my practiced fingers. With the station in tiptop shape, the ladder truck and ambulance gleaming in their bays, and Dobbs on kitchen duty, I've roped in a couple of the other guys for a game of poker with chores for chips.

"Shuffle all you want, but I'm still gonna win," Samuels, a retired pro football player, snickers.

The Leaning Tower of Pisa stack of chips he's guarding with a mallet-sized fist warns me I've been had. "I thought you said you only played poker a couple of times?"

His teeth rival the chrome bumper of the firetruck

for brilliance. "Should have said a few, huh? Come on, Fraser, deal them out. I need my bedding changed."

I glance at the third in our mismatched trio, Fredericks, and shudder. Give me a broken bone or a bloody gash over a grungy set of sheets laden with skin cells and who knows what else—yuck.

Fredericks chuckles at my reaction, his reading glasses hooked by the bump on the end of his patrician nose. "Don't look at me, I'm about to cash out and try some of that firehouse chili Dobbs is cooking."

The aroma coming from the kitchen is mouthwatering and for a hopeful moment it looks as though Samuels might follow suit, but then he taps two sausage-like fingers on the table. "Deal, brother, clock's tickin'."

Sighing, I send his cards gliding across the steel tabletop and lift mine, corner up first, each one worse than the last. A pair of fives. "You've got to be kidding me."

"What are you muttering? Bad hand, buddy? Want to fold now and quit while you're behind? Oh, wait, too late." Samuels slaps a thick thigh and laughs uproariously.

"Your comedian skills need work." I scowl and wait for him to make his bet.

"Fraser, you have a visitor." The captain raises

bushy eyebrows at the card game, then nods over his shoulder. "She's out front."

Hiding a relieved sigh, I toss my pair face-up and chuckle at Samuels. "Sorry, man, next time."

"I'll wait. We're here all day." Samuels grins good-naturedly and picks up the deck to shuffle the cards.

I could tell him I'm leaving early for a funeral but don't. It would take too long to explain my need to attend the service in support of an ex-girlfriend. I just do.

The service bay fills me with a deep sense of pride. I've worked hard to get to where I am, and while there are heartbreaking aspects to the job—like the young girl, Nicole, whose parents are so busy blaming each other they fail to hear their daughter's silent cry for help—there are rewards, as well. I want to tell Renée it was her father's death that changed my life and gave it purpose, but the cost to her family was steep and I'm afraid I'll only hurt her with my inadequate words.

I'm surprised to see Izzy wearing a hole in the drive outside the bay doors, head down, red hair dampened by a light drizzle, bunched into a messy bun on the back of her neck. But it's the look she gives me as I step out the door that freezes me in my tracks, my heart plummeting to my toes. We've been here before, she and I. It was raining then, too. The night Renée ran away from me and her family, she instantly destroyed the dream I'd carried of building a life and growing old with her.

I should have known she'd do it again.

"When did she leave?" I ask, unable to mask the resignation in my voice.

Izzy stares at me, confusion clouding stormy blue eyes. Memories stir and for a moment, it's as though we're caught up in some weird kind of déjà vu. Bound together by love and loss—her for her sister, me for my best friend and lover. My soul mate.

She shakes her head, hurrying toward me, and grasping my hands with icy fingers. "Not Renée, not this time. It's Benjamin. I went to check on him this morning and his bed wasn't slept in. I've searched everywhere, then I thought of how he looks up to you and raced over hoping you'd be here." Her freckles stood out like a roadmap of fear, turning her skin alabaster and lips pale except for where she'd gnawed on the bottom one, causing it to swell. "Have you talked to him, Simon? Do you know where my little brother is?"

My heart squeezes for her. Hasn't she been through enough? "Slow down," I say, trying to calm the escalating panic I can feel zapping through her body. "Are you sure he's not at a friend's house? You know

how kids are, they don't always think before they do."
Mom was always telling me I gave her gray hairs as a
teen because I'd forget to let her in on my plans.

"I called them. No one has heard from him in
days," she cries, tears making her eyes look like deep
pools of despair. "I'm supposed to be at the funeral
home getting everything ready for the service, and now
this. I don't know what to do."

I pull her in for a gentle embrace, trying to impart
reassurance though I'm not sure what I can do. I've
talked to Renée's brother on a few occasions, but we
aren't close. I'm not even sure where kids hang out
these days, then the river comes to mind and chills
creep up my spine.

I lean back to meet her gaze. "Does Benjamin like
to go tubing on the river?" It's running higher than
normal this year thanks to a rainy spring, creating
streamflow advisories and the danger of submerged
deadfalls waiting to trap the unwary.

"Of course, we all do. But he wouldn't go today,
would he?" She pulls free, turning toward the road and
her vintage VW Beetle. "He's grounded for life when I
find him."

"Wait," I call. "I'll go with you. Just let me clear it
with the captain." The last thing we need is to be
rescuing not one, but two, bodies from the Chinook on
the eve of their mother's funeral.

She raises a hand in acknowledgment, climbing behind the wheel of her car. I rush inside, explain the situation, get a stern warning to call if anything goes sideways, and jog back to where I left her, but Izzy has driven away.

CHAPTER TWENTY-ONE

RENÉE

Choosing a dress for a parent's funeral shouldn't be on anyone's list of must-do's. I'd brought the staid black knee-length I bought for Dad's funeral—and never wore—but couldn't bring myself to slip into it today. Mom deserves more, a dress that shows how much she meant to me while growing up in a house of cards. *One wrong move and they all fall down.*

Defiant, I pluck the flowered sundress off its hanger and lay it across the end of the bed. The giant peonies in shades of raspberry and pink blend with the old-fashioned quilt Mrs. O'Brian told me she stitched while her husband was deployed overseas. When she spoke of him, her eyes turned soft with love and hazy with memories of times gone by. So very different from my parents.

Mom admitted once after a particularly abrasive argument with my dad that they'd gotten married after finding out she was pregnant—with me. The guilt from her confession burrowed deep into my heart, and I'm afraid it's affected every relationship I've had since. If nothing else, three years of psychology classes and cognitive therapy have taught me how to deal with my emotional hang-ups and move forward.

Starting with this dress.

I want to celebrate the mom who skipped rope with her daughters, made the best birthday cakes, read us to sleep, and made bunny pancakes with strawberry noses in the morning. The woman she was before life wore her down and took away her dreams.

A glance out the window shows pewter clouds trapped on the towering hemlocks flanking the horizon. *Tears from Heaven,* Mom used to say. The angels are surely weeping today.

I haven't heard from Izzy and assume I'll meet her and Benjamin at the funeral home. I wish she would have allowed me to help with the preparations. She's too independent for her own good. I knew it would be a no, so I sent an anonymous donation to cover the cost of the service and ordered an arrangement of lilies for the casket. We're a family, it's time we started acting like one.

Dressed, I tread down the staircase, my hand gliding over the polished banister. The closer it gets to the service, the more it feels as though a leaden balloon is growing in my chest—when it breaks, I'll be lost.

Stopping at my patient's bedroom door, I tap lightly on the wood panel. "Mrs. O'Brian, may I come in?"

Bedcovers rustle from the other side of the partially open door, and she bids me to enter. "Good morning, dear," she says, her voice quivering as she tries to lift up on her elbows but falls back with a soft whoomph. "You look pretty today. Are you going on a date?"

"Thank you. It's my mother's funeral actually." I hurry forward to place a fluffy pillow behind her head, hiding my concern at the towering stack of tissues on her bedside table. "How do you feel today?"

"Other than weak and ineffectual, you mean?" She grimaces. "Don't get old, dear. It's for the birds."

I chuckle. "I only hope I can be as active as you in my golden years. Simon is lucky to have you."

She grasps my hand with hers, the skin incredibly soft and frail. "My grandson is a good boy, even if he is rather blind in some matters." She winks, as though sharing a secret. "But it's not too late for him... and for you."

I gasp and pull away, surprised by her boldness. "Mrs. O'Brian, Simon is engaged. I'd say that's too late, even if I did want to get back together with him—which I don't. I'm happy for him. Really, I am."

She gives me a knowing look and I see where her grandson gets his obstinacy. "Whatever you say, dear. Now, are you going to help me find a dress to compliment yours for your mother's send-off?"

Overwhelmed with affection for this kind, sweet lady, I give her an impulsive hug, closing my eyes to breathe in the lilac scent of her hair tickling my cheek. "Yes, ma'am."

She pats my back and whispers in my ear. "Your mother would be proud of you, child. Hold her love in your heart."

Swallowing hard, I nod and turn toward her closet, surreptitiously swiping at the first of what will be many tears today. "So, will it be the purple print or rose silk?"

The house phone sets up a strident ring and I gasp, my nerves on edge. Mrs. O'Brian answers, lifting the instrument to her ear. "Yes?" she says, overloud, probably because her hearing isn't the best. Her eyes widen, and she quickly holds the receiver out to me. "She says she's your sister. Something is wrong."

My heart seizes, then goes into overdrive

—*Benjamin.*

Fingers trembling, I take the phone, my voice shaky. "Y...yes?"

"Ben is missing," Izzy sobs. "I was going through his bag—"

"Why were you snooping in Ben's things?" I can barely understand her. None of this is making sense.

"—and when I checked in on him, his bed was empty. He never came home last night, Renée." Her panic comes through the line, amping up my own misgivings.

"He probably stayed at a friend's. Have you called around?" I wish the words back the moment it leaves my lips. Of course, she would have gotten hold of anyone she could think of and now she's going to think I'm questioning her common sense. "Izz..."

"Never mind," she mutters. "I should have known better, but Simon insisted I call."

Simon? What does he have to do with this, and what is he doing with my sister?

"Wait, don't hang up. I'm sorry. Now, where are you? I'll come over and we can search for him together, okay?"

Mrs. O'Brian stares at me with furrowed brows and grasps my hand.

"We're nearing the Chinook swimming hole. I've looked everywhere else. You can meet us here. Hurry,

Renée. I'm scared." The line goes dead, and I'm left clutching at hope. I can't lose another member of my family, I just can't.

CHAPTER TWENTY-TWO

RENÉE

The Chinook Parking lot is empty except for a couple of pickups, my sister's vintage VW, and Simon's distinctive green Barracuda. My breath hitches in my throat. All the way across town, driving Mrs. O'Brian's fancy sedan at speeds it probably has never seen, I've tried to convince myself it's all a mistake. That Ben is playing a trick on my sister and is simply hiding in his closet under his clothes the way he used to as a child. But Benjamin isn't a baby anymore and it's hammered home that his disappearance is all too real.

I park next to Simon's car and try to call Izzy, but there's no reply. Rain coats the windshield in a filmy mist that distorts the view up and down the swollen river and treed hills beyond.

flipping the hood up on my UC Berkeley sweatshirt, I climb out of the borrowed vehicle, grateful Mrs. O'Brian's neighbor was able to stay with her and shiver from a combination of nerves and the cool wind blowing across the water.

After double-checking whether I'd locked the doors, I throw the keys and my phone in the front pouch and work my way down to the trail that runs parallel to the river. For a stunned moment, I stare at the drab olive caldron swirling by, shocked by the change in a river known for its lazy nature and gentle eddies. Water like this can suck a person under and wash them miles downstream, leaving their broken bodies hung up in the deadfall gathered like discarded twigs against the banks.

My little brother could be drowning as I stand here debating which way to search. Shrugging off the terrifying thought, I stumble upriver calling Benjamin's name every few feet, though the wind, rain, and snarling water eat my words almost before they leave my trembling lips.

Where is he? Where are Izzy and Simon? The remoteness of the area has my pulse jumping at every little noise, from pebbles bouncing down the hill I just skidded down, to swaying branches scraping each other as the storm intensifies. The well-worn trail is a mix of clay and gravel and is quickly becoming treacherous to navigate in my flimsy sandals.

I stop to get my bearings, blinking rain and tears out of my eyes. There's a bend in the river ahead of me and I realize I'm at the spot teens call Kissing Hollow for the natural overhang of the bank and a sandy beach, allowing young lovers a measure of privacy for their rendezvous.

Hope rising, I hurry toward the hideaway, shouting for Ben, but no one answers, the area is deserted, though empty beer cans and a smoldering fire alert me to the fact I'm not as alone as it feels out here.

Hugging myself for comfort, as well as warmth, I debate the safety of continuing down the trail. I might not even be going the right way. Simon, Izzy, and Ben could even now be heading back to town, not realizing I'm the one needing saving if the beer drinkers find me.

Giving the bend a regretful glance, I turn to make my way down the trail when a faint sound arrests me in my tracks. Is that...?

"Izzy! Izz, where are you?" I stumble and go down hard on one knee, ripping skin on the rough ground, but barely acknowledge the injury, my focus on the misty path in front of me.

Scrambling to my feet, I curse the flimsy sandals

I'm wearing and kick them aside to break into a full-out run, wincing as pebbles that feel like boulders stub my toes and bruise the balls of my feet. It doesn't matter, nothing matters except getting to my family in time—unlike the night I let my dad die.

Rounding the curve in the track, I gasp. My heart stutters. Izzy—who doesn't know how to swim—is waist-deep in the fast-flowing water, barely maintaining her balance while holding a long, flimsy branch toward a toppled tree, half-buried in the brackish stream.

Then I see him. Benjamin is lodged under a thick branch, his face a white blur rising and falling at the whim of a capricious current, thin arms struggling to grasp a too-thick trunk.

Knowing every moment could be his last, I yank the hoodie over my head, drop it on the bank, and race for the water, sucking in a surprised gasp at the icy coldness. "Hold on, Ben. Don't let go."

I startle Izzy, who almost goes down herself, arms flailing to stay upright, and I'm forced to detour and help her first.

"Hang on, Izz. I've got you." I get behind her and grasp her waist until she stabilizes herself, then take the stick and throw it downstream where it tumbles and disappears with the current.

"Hey," she stutters, her teeth clacking. "We... we need to hel... help Benjamin."

I brush the sodden hair out of her face and make her look at me. "I want you to *carefully* make your way back to shore. There's a cellphone in my hoodie, call 911 if you can get any service. It was spotty earlier. I'm going to swim to Ben and see how he's doing."

Her eyes are glazed. She most likely is in the early stages of hypothermia, but I need her to listen, so I give her a rough shake and receive a glare in return.

"Quit that. I can barely stay up as it is. He's my responsibility—I'm staying." Her lips have a blue tinge, but she still manages a mulish pout.

"I don't have time to argue about this. Just do what I ask, will you?" I break away from her and throw my body into the water, grateful for the log keeping my brother afloat and the current at bay, though I can still feel it tugging at my legs like a siren of the deep come to take my soul.

"Where's Simon?" I gasp, in between strokes, my breathing harsh in my ears.

"He took the other direction, so we could cover more ground. Hurry, he's slipping," she screams.

Sure enough, I glance up in time to see Ben's arms drop and his head slide under the waves buffeting the tree trunk. If he gets dragged below the debris, I'll lose him, I know it. Shifting to a power stroke, I dig deep, my lungs a battering ram in my chest. But it's not enough. Just as I get close enough to reach out and grab his jacket, my brother slides out of my grasp and disappears into the murky depths.

CHAPTER TWENTY-THREE

SIMON

The rain picks up steam the further down the trail I get, making the terrain treacherous. The wind must be gusting close to twenty miles an hour, battering the trees and creating whitecaps on the swollen river overflowing its bank on my left. The park should be closed until the runoff retreats, I'm surprised it hasn't been—though it wouldn't stop a kid trying to escape a parent's funeral.

Guilt dogs my steps. Ben reached out to me the night I took Renée home and I let it slide. If I'd been there for him, maybe we wouldn't be out here in this shit storm searching for him. Renée must be out of her mind right now. Izzy's frantic call would have sent her racing to the rescue, that's Renée's way—she's a caregiver.

It will destroy those girls if their brother doesn't come home. I can't let that happen.

There's been no sign of him so far, though the rain is wiping the ground clean, erasing any trace of human activity other than the odd can laying discarded alongside the path. I hope Izzy's having more luck on her end. I didn't like letting her go alone but conceded it was the smart thing to do—splitting up will cover a greater area in case the kid is injured. I remember my pre-teen years, girls suddenly take on a new appeal. Their bodies transition from chubby cuteness to eye-popping splendor. Meanwhile, males go through growing pains that shoot through legs and hips as bones stretch and reshape themselves, while hormones flare at uncomfortable times as testosterone levels increase, creating mood swings, aggression, and even depression.

It's the last one that worries me the most. Benjamin has been through more than any child should, with the suicide of his father, and now his mother's passing. He must feel lost, unsure of what the future will mean for him and his sisters. Izzy is barely old enough to care for herself, never mind raising a willful teen, and Renée will be going back to her career and the bright city lights. Our little town—I—couldn't hold her here before, it's doubtful she'll stay this time, either. It doesn't matter, marrying Lacey would be wrong. I love her, she's everything I thought I wanted in a wife, but she's not Renée. Just thinking about my ex makes my heart squeeze in a way it's never done for my fiancée. The first time I kissed those full, pouty lips it transported me to another dimension. I knew then she was the one. Too bad she didn't feel the same.

A rivulet of cold rain drips down the nape of my neck, jerking me back to the present and the two men stumbling toward me out of the woods.

"Hey," I call, waving my arms to get their attention. "Have you guys seen a kid out here?"

The men amble over, silly smirks on their faces, jackets undone, and a beer in their hands. "Ahoy, mate," The taller one says, a swagger in his step. "Nice night for a pint or three, don't you agree?'

The other guy laughs uproariously, stringy blond hair slapping the side of his baby face. He shoulder bumps his buddy and they almost go down in a drunken pile. "Awesome, man. You could write a country song with that line."

Great, a couple of idiots. "This is important. A young boy is missing and could be in extreme danger. I'm going to ask you again, have you seen a kid wandering around out here on his own, or haven't you?" I don't have time for their foolishness, every minute is crucial.

The tall one straightens and shrugs out of his friend's hold. "Sorry, man, we're just goofing off. There was a teen a while back. We were upriver, had a little fire going and a few brewskis—not too many," he hurries to add, staring at my uniform. "He asked if he could warm up. Said he was thirsty, so we gave him a beer—it's all we had—and told him to get lost when he asked for another."

My hands fist and I lunge forward, but he takes a hasty step sideways and pinwheels his arms after tripping over his buddy's feet.

"I'm sorry, man. How were we to know the punk ran away? We didn't do anything wrong."

"Nothing except feeding a minor alcohol. You two are lucky I have a child to find, or I'd cuff you here until the authorities arrive. Now, get out of my sight. And you better not be planning on driving anytime soon, or I *will* have you arrested, got it?"

They look too out of it to realize I'm an EMT, not a cop. They pick themselves up and scramble down the trail, probably intending to walk to the bridge and thumb a ride to town. I pull my phone out and curse at the no signal indicator—damn weather. It's always catch-and-miss service along the river, but I was hoping to catch a break. No such luck. The park is about twenty miles wide and twice that long, encompassing the Chinook River, foothills leading into the Cascade

Mountains, dangerous wildlife, and rocky terrain. Any of it a threat to man, never mind an angry teen with nothing left to lose. The hopelessness of it overwhelms me, but the vision of Izzy's desperate face won't let me give up.

I turn and jog toward the area the men said they last saw Ben, praying I'm not too late.

CHAPTER TWENTY-FOUR

RENÉE

The water is murky, filled with sediment and debris siphoned up from the river bottom. It's like sandpaper, chafing my arms and burning my eyes, making it hard to see anything more than the snag with its snarl of limbs stretching diagonal to the fast-flowing stream.

After only a few strokes my arms ache, the under-current stronger than I ever remember it. I glance over my shoulder to make sure Izzy made it out safely and catch a glimpse of her kneeling next to my hoodie, phone in hand, her fear-filled gaze on the rescue mission. My head lightens with relief—or is that a lack of oxygen?—knowing she's on dry land. Now to help my brother.

Benjamin's frightened face pops up, his gasps loud and panic-stricken, arms flailing for purchase before he slides under a partially submerged bough. Terrified I won't reach him in time, I kick harder, diving under the last few feet to push through the wall of water slowing my efforts.

The branch materializes right in front of me, and I run full force into it, rattling my teeth. Rough bark scrapes the left side of my face, burning my cheek as I glide underneath. It's dark and eerie and I want nothing more than to escape this nightmare, push my way out and breathe ozone-rich air, but not until I find Ben.

Hands out, I feel my way along, sweeping moss and twigs out of my way, and barely withholding a scream when old man's beard brushes ethereal fingers across my skin. *Where is he?* My lungs deflate, bubbles tickling my lips, and know I can't stay here much longer. Pulse sluggish, I bump into something and lethargically reach out to move it out of my way and encounter cloth. *Benjamin.*

Filled with a new sense of purpose, I grasp the material and tug but, other than a slight give, nothing happens. *He's trapped!*

Frantic, I trace what turns out to be his arm up to the shoulder and find his head lolling forward, dark hair washing back and forth like seaweed with the stirred-up water. In danger of passing out myself, I wrap a hand around his back, burrowing my fingers into his underarm, and yank with every ounce of remaining strength I have.

Nothing.

Heartsick, left with no choice, I lean over to give his cold cheek a watery kiss, turn to duck under the branch, and swim to the surface, gasping for air.

Sobbing, I pull myself high enough to see Izzy and start to cry in earnest when Simon's determined face breaks the surface just a few feet away.

"H... here," I croak, waving a wet noodle that passes for my arm in the air. "Help."

"Are you alright?" He treads water near me, eyes grim. "You scared the hell out of me."

"It's... Ben," I rasp, my throat raw. "He's... trapped. I couldn't get him free."

Simon gives a sharp nod. "Stay here, hold onto the tree branch. Don't let go. I can't lose you, Renée, I won't survive. Don't worry, honey, I'll bring your brother back to you."

His lips graze mine and then he's gone, diving into the watery tomb imprisoning my brother. The rain beats on my head and drips in my eyes, but I barely notice, my sole focus on the opaque river hiding her secrets from me. How long can a person go without breathing? I feel like we learned the answer in school—

or was it in lifeguard classes?—but I can't remember now. Three minutes? Four? Brain damage is first, then the organs shut down one by one until death takes over. It's been at least two minutes, maybe more. He can't go much longer. I haven't been to church in years, but I pray now. I pray *He* saves my brother and protects Simon. I pray for second chances and lost family bonds. I pray until the water boils around my legs and Benjamin breaks the surface, his body pushed up like a torpedo, Simon's hand fisted into the waistband of his sodden jeans.

Heart thundering, I do my best to keep his head above water, but unconscious it's akin to stopping a boulder from rolling down a mountain. Thankfully, Simon takes over, turning Ben so he's on his back with Simon's arm under his chin, hand gripping his shoulder to keep him afloat.

"I have to get him to shore, there's no time to waste. Stay here, I'll come back for you as soon as I can." His gaze implores me to listen even though it's *my brother* and he could be dying as we speak. "Baby, please? I need to know you're safe so I can do my job."

Everything within urges me to take over, power through the river, and save my brother's life, though I know I can't—I'm not strong enough. But Simon is. He'll get Benjamin to shore and perform the necessary

CPR to resuscitate him in time. Please, God, let him get there in time.

He meets my gaze and for some reason, I'm reassured by the warmth in his. "Go, I'll wait."

The trip to shore seems to take forever. Simon keeps a steady pace, though he has to be tired with the effort of tugging my brother's deadweight through the cantankerous current. When they are close enough, Izzy runs out and between the two of them, they get Ben to the bank where Simon immediately begins CPR. He yanks the jacket open and puts his ear to Benjamin's chest, then tips his chin up, pinches his nose shut, and blows two sharp breaths into his mouth, before starting chest compressions while Izzy stands to the side wringing her hands. My skin is numb but it's nothing compared to the piercing agony attacking my heart the longer Ben lies there with no response.

Just as I begin to fear I didn't get to him fast enough, Ben jerks up and rolls to his side, coughing and choking as the river drains from his lungs. The tears and guilt I've carried since witnessing Dad falling to the ground, half of his head blown off, overflows, mingling with the cleansing rain. *He's alive.*

"Mom, Dad, if you're up there I'm going to be a better sister to Benjamin and Izzy. I've been given a second chance and I'm not going to waste it. No more running, I promise."

First responders jog into view and quickly take over Ben's care, checking his vitals and preparing him for the spineboard they've brought with them. Simon points toward me and one of the men slaps him on the back before removing what looks like an emergency blanket from his kit.

Izzy stops hovering over Ben long enough to hurry to the shore. "He's talking, Renée. You saved him."

I raise my hand, grateful beyond words for *His* blessing on our brother's life. Just then the rain eases and a streak of light breaks through the clouds, its benevolent rays penetrating the murky river, turning it into a thing of beauty. Life is full of challenges; it's how we handle them that makes us the people we are.

CHAPTER TWENTY-FIVE

SIMON

The trip to the parking lot is silent, Renée and I lost in the traumatic events of the day. Now that my adrenalin is fading, the chill from wet clothes and windy conditions has goosebumps erupting on every inch of exposed skin, and shivers wrack my body. I glance over to see how she's making out and frown. She's trudging along, head down, exhausted. Her tremors make the emergency blanket shimmer and rustle with every step.

I come to a standstill and present my hunched-over back. "Hop on."

"What?" She stumbles to a halt and gasps, startled laughter erasing some of the pensiveness from her expression.

"Hop on, I'll give you a lift." When she hesitates, I wriggle my brows suggestively. "Come on, it's not like it's our first time."

Color washes over her cheeks, making me grin at the same time it brings up memories of other firsts I've shared with this woman. She was the first girl I actively pursued as a teen. I was a football jock, girls liked me. Not Renée though. She was too busy getting good grades to pay attention to the high school football team. We were complete opposites, but I didn't let that stop me. I was fascinated by the studious blonde and made it a mission to know her. It took some convincing, but she gave me a chance, and soon we were seeing each other exclusively—something new for me. She took me home to meet her parents: another first, and awkward as hell. Her dad was a big brute of a guy, with a right curve to his nose and black beads for eyes over hedge-like brows. Her mom, on the other hand, was shy and welcoming: slight like her daughters with a darker shade of blonde hair than Renée. Dinner was one of those affairs nightmares are made of stilted conversation, barely veiled warnings, and a pesky younger sister determined to cause trouble—not exactly Hallmark movie quality. But it was also the night for another first: making love. Oh, I'd had my misadventures in the sex department, I was seventeen after all. But what happened between Renée and me in the backseat of my old Chevy Nova, scared me to death. Suddenly, we weren't just playing at being a couple, I became committed. She was it for me. The only girl I wanted. The one I planned to spend the rest of my life making love to, having babies with. Except she wasn't on the same page as me. When she left, I was lost.

Now she's back and I'm dreaming of forever again —talk about a glutton for punishment.

"It's no big deal, okay? I just happen to be built stronger than you. Take advantage of it and let me help you to the car so we can get to the hospital." I exaggerate my shivers. "Besides, I'm cold, and you're frozen. My car has a furnace for a heating system. The sooner we get there, the sooner we can dry off." I'd suggest stripping out of our wet clothes, but it would go over like a lead balloon, though the visual has steam rising from my pants.

She gives my back a misgiving look, then carefully drapes herself around me like my favorite blanket and I have to close my eyes for a minute to let the sensations wash over me. Even though we're both clammy and dirty from the silty river, her arms are soft and silky where they brush against my neck. The cushion of her breasts pressed against my shoulder blades has me fighting the urge to drop to my knees, roll her under me, and prove what we had is still alive. Instead, I grasp her thighs, hoisting her up so she rests on my waist, bare legs dangling like wet noodles.

"Wrap your legs around my hips, it'll be easier for both of us." Maybe not for my sanity, but I can deal with it. My main concern is getting her warm. Hypothermia occurs when the body drops to ninety-five degrees or lower and can creep up unexpectedly, causing damage to the heart and nervous system. Renée is showing signs of the symptoms: shivering, slurred words, shallow breathing, clumsiness, and very low energy. I'm not sure how long she was in the water before I arrived, but the blue tinge to her lips is worrying.

By the time we get to the car, the rain has stopped though the wind continues to howl through the trees, chilling me to the bone. The only other vehicles in the lot are Grams' Cadillac, parked next to the 'Cuda, and Izzy's car. She must have caught a ride in the ambulance. I'll have to pick the Cadillac up later, Renée is in no condition to drive.

I unlock the doors with my key fob and carefully lower her to the ground, catching her by the arm when she loses balance. She stares up at me, her blue eyes wide and as lustrous as the sapphires in her ears.

Hot.

"Simon..."

The way she looks at me steals my breath. Without

thought, I lower my head and sink into the vortex of lust and need I've always felt since the first time our lips met. She lets out a little sigh, the sensation so erotic my dick jumps in response. I've wanted this woman forever, and now that she's here, in my arms, I'm never letting go. I'm filled with the compulsion to devour, to convey without words how much she means to me, but I force myself to slow down, nibbling my way along her jaw, then back to her mouth, drawn like a magnet to the moistness within.

Her arms ribbon my neck, her fingers delving into my hair, caressing my nape, sending carnal need flashing up my spine. I growl and capture her waist, drawing our bodies flush to each other from chest to thigh. The emergency blanket slips to the ground, but I barely notice other than to make sure we don't trip on the thing. I have a brief moment of clarity and lift my head to ask Renée if she's okay. If she's sure this is what she wants, but I'm distracted by the sight of her nipples poking through the thin material of her dress.

"Are you cold?" I murmur. Cupping their fullness in my hands, I brush my thumb over the nub and smile at the responding tremor.

"N...no," she stammers, her fingers icy as they drop to my wrists. "Don't stop."

Shit, what am I doing? I'm an EMT, damn it. I *know* the consequences of stress and hypothermia, yet

I still chose to feed my baser instincts instead of caring for the woman I love more than life. I'm a jerk.

"We have to." I meld my hips to hers to show how much it hurts me to let her go and reach for the discarded wrap. "You're freezing. Let's get in the car. We need to talk."

She frowns, but complies, dragging the silver sheet around her as though it's a barrier to something she doesn't want to hear. Too bad. I'm not letting her run away from me again. If she won't live here, I'll move. Nothing matters more than Renée. I should have followed her years ago. I'm not going to make the same mistake.

If she wants me.

CHAPTER TWENTY-SIX

RENÉE

I huddle into the crinkly emergency blanket and wait for the heat pouring out of the vents to warm me while trying to ignore the exasperating man sitting in the driver's seat. What started as a quest for comfort flared into an incendiary fire between us. Now that it is over, guilt, regret, and concern for my brother are roiling in my stomach like a toxic stew.

Simon wants to talk and is probably even now searching for a way to let me down gently. *"You're great, but this is a mistake. We were carried away by the moment, it isn't real. We aren't a couple anymore. I care about you, Renée."* I can hear it all now and wish I could disappear. Go back in time to when we were young and in love and the world was our oyster. Before my world imploded.

"That feels better," he says, reaching in front of me to direct the vents higher, sending warm air flowing toward my side of the car. My skin tingles as though waking from a long nap, then begins to burn, searing my face and arms; dragging me into the here and now and a conversation I don't want to endure.

"We should go, I'm worried about Benjamin." I put my hands, palm out, to the heat, sighing with relief at the warmth.

"He's in good hands. Your brother is lucky you came along, it could have gone much differently." Turning slightly, he rests against the door and studies me like a specimen under a microscope.

"What?" I snap, shifting uncomfortably. He's always had this steady gaze that seems to see inside of me, to the introvert who is afraid of conflict and would rather put her head in the sand than cause a scene.

"I'm not going to marry Lacey if you're wondering." He reaches for my hand and meshes our fingers together—a bridge that can't be broken unless we allow it to. "I love you, Renée. I've always loved you, and I think you feel the same. I want a second chance to make things right between us."

Make things right.

I want that too, more than I can express. But how

can I ever wholly trust someone with my heart after witnessing the debacle of my parent's marriage? A marriage that ended in death?

"Simon, it's... complicated. The night we broke up, seeing you in that girl's arms was hard. I thought we had something special—"

"We did, baby. You didn't give me a chance to explain—"

I try to break loose of his hold, but he won't let go and for some reason, this angers me. I lift my chin and stare him in the eye as I bare my soul for the first time since therapy. "Did you know pulling a trigger under your chin doesn't necessarily kill you right away?

There's a sick satisfaction to the shock he shows. His jaw slackens and his eyes widen, then squint as though he feels my dad's agony after the bullet ripped away half of his face.

"I was there. I ran home after you... anyway, I wanted to be alone and thought I'd sit in the backyard for a while, watch the stars and think of ways to get out of this town. But, as I opened the gate, I saw Dad. He was just standing there, staring at the ground, all alone.

"I think I backed up to give him privacy, but I tripped over one of Benjamin's toys. He always left them scattered all over the yard even though Mom threatened to throw them away—damn kid. Dad heard me and turned, and that's when I saw the gun. He had it kind of lodged under his chin. I thought it was a freaking tie for a minute. I mean, it was graduation, and they were supposed to come to the supper, right? How was I to know he was in our backyard getting up the nerve to kill himself instead of sitting at a table full of proud parents bragging about their incredibly smart children and their accomplishments? No, once again my dad had to make it all about him." I'm babbling, I know I am, but I can't seem to stop now that the rot that fermented inside of me for years is finally set free.

"Renée, sweetheart." Simon reaches to take me in his arms, but I lurch back, determined to get it all out in the open. Every. Last. Deplorable second.

"Wait, you haven't heard the best part. You see, I must have startled him and his finger pressed the trigger at the same time as he started to lower the gun, so instead of shooting himself in the brain and ending it quickly, the bullet ripped through his jaw, taking his mouth, nose, cheek, and eye before exiting through the top of his forehead. I know because I tried to save him." I'm crying now, messy, gulping sobs that make it hard to finish. To get the story out so I never have to say or dream it again.

Simon ignores my stiff body and pulls me over the console and onto his lap, his hand cradling my head as I give in to the guilt and agony I've carried for too long. "Shh," he murmurs, raining kisses on my eyes, cheeks, and lips, drawing away the sorrow and replacing it with something closer to peace. "I've got you. You don't have to go through this alone anymore. I'm here and I'm not going anywhere, honey. I've got you."

The words slide under my skin and heal all the broken pieces inside. I'm not sure if I can ever fully forgive myself for causing Dad to pull the trigger, but deep inside I know Simon won't let me flounder. And really, that's all I can ask for: love isn't always easy, and sometimes it can lead to despair, but when it's right... when it's right it makes life worth living.

CHAPTER TWENTY-SEVEN

IZZY

This time when Renée arrives, I'm ready for her and open the door before she can knock. "Simon Fraser, huh?" I waggle my brows as he honks and drives away with a wave of the hand.

Her cheeks pick up a rosy hue as she leans in to hug me. Surprised, I don't know what to do with my arms at first. They hang at my side like sagging ropes, but then the warmth of her body, the fact my sister is *here* after risking her life to save our brother last week, brings life to my limbs. I embrace her waist, awkwardly at first, then tighter as though she's my port in a storm, and in a way, she is. Burying my face in her neck I breathe in the mingling scents of magnolia and peaches —Mom's favorite.

"Are you okay?" she murmurs, rubbing my back in a soothing motion that quiets the turmoil in my breast.

"Sure. The funeral was nice, wasn't it?" I reluctantly let go, stepping aside to let her in. It feels like déjà vu except I'm not stomping down the hall in a fit—I'll take that as progress.

She nods and fingers a bouquet of white roses on the entry table. "It was a good turnout. Where's Benjamin?"

I lead the way to the kitchen and start a pot of coffee to have something to do with my hands. "He's at Scott's. I thought it would be good for him to hang out with his friend."

"You're probably right. Any side effects from the drowning?" She sets her purse on the table and wanders around the room, touching Mom's wallpaper, staring at the kindergarten picture Ben painted that I had framed and hung next to the olive-green fridge we'd had for as long as I could remember.

"Seems fine, but you know Ben—" I drop my gaze to the drip-drip of elixir falling into the glass carafe. How could she know what he was like now? She's barely seen him in the last two years. The cute kid she remembers is gone, replaced by a morose, defiant stranger.

"I want to," she says, enfolding my fingers. "I'm sorry, Izz. I should have been here for you. I'm not going to make excuses; I just want a chance to make it up to you—both of you."

She squeezes my hand, then moves away to take a seat at the table. "I thought you might like to know I'm opening a therapy practice downtown." She smiles at my startled surprise. "I told you; I'm not running away anymore. It won't be much, to begin with, but Simon is helping. He has a young girl he'd like me to work with and a few other possible patients. It might take a while, but I plan to pitch in around here, and support Benjamin."

I stiffen. "What does that mean? Ben is mine, Renée. He's all I've got left and I'm not letting him go." I may be young and possibly unemployed soon, but none of that matters. Other single parents have made it work, I will too.

"You've been amazing," she says, leaning forward as though I'll listen better if her big blue eyes are in my face. "But it's my turn now. I've done my traveling, received a degree I'm proud of, and am reconciling with Simon." That sappy smile again. "Don't you want the same opportunities?"

She looks at me expectantly, as though I'm a lapdog waiting for a walk in the park. I won't deny I'm worried about Ben, social services, and the weird drawing from his backpack, but that doesn't make me my sister. I'm not running away just because things aren't going my way.

"Well, this has been fun. I always enjoy a good teardown of my character. I realize you *think* you've accomplished a miraculous change, but while you were away playing at adulthood I was here caring for our dying mother and little brother." I grab the full coffeepot and dump the steaming liquid down the sink, fuming. "You have *no* idea what that was like: giving Mom sponge baths when she became too weak to shower. Changing her bedpan. Watching her fade away and not being able to stop it, no matter how hard I prayed. Wishing my big sister was here to help shoulder the responsibilities, to pay the bills and drive Ben to school and cook and clean, and a hundred other jobs we all took for granted as kids."

I clench my hands on the cool rim of the sink and take a deep breath, fighting for control. "If you want Ben, you'll have to fight me for him. Other than that, we have nothing else to say."

I listen as Renée slowly stands, the tattletale squeal of her chair on the battered yellow lino. *Please, just go.*

Instead, she crosses the room and places a gentle hand on my shoulder. "We're sisters, not enemies. I love you, Izzy. I won't let you push me out of your lives. Call me when you want to talk."

And then she was gone, and the empty house settled around me as the tears splashed down the drain.

COMING SPRING 2023

FINDING ME: THE DEFIANT SISTERS-
BOOK 2

Prologue

Izzy

The day my life changed forever started like any other. Mom yelling for me to get out of bed, my sister hogging all the hot water in the shower, and my little brother peeping at me from the doorway to my room.

"Beat it, creep," I mumble, throwing my one good pillow at his head. He grins and takes off for the stairs as fast as his still-pudgy little legs will carry him. I sigh and flop onto my back, blinking the sleep from my eyes. Dust motes floated in the air through the early morning rays of the sun sneaking past my half-closed blinds. Upstairs, the floorboards creak as Mom moves around the kitchen preparing our lunches. That nagging cough of hers grosses me out. It's a cross between a gag and a snort; real attractive first thing in the morning.

A vibration under my right shoulder blade has me doing a frantic search for my cell through the topsy-turvy mess I'd made of my blankets. The *Hello Kitty* case shakes again. I turn it over to find five messages from my best friend, Trinity.

Did you decide yet?

It's going to be a blast!!!

The biggest party of the year, and it's your birthday □

Kyle's going

Izzy, are you there?

Kyle's going? Oh, man. Trinity teased me, but Kyle is the cutest boy in ninth grade and nice, too. Ever since he'd turned to me in Hendricks's class and asked for help with Canada's social and economic growth and the connection to natural resources, I'd been dreaming of those dark brown eyes. I needed to go to that party.

What are you going to wear?

Knowing Trinity, she'd probably shopped all weekend for the perfect outfit.

I found the perfect outfit! Wait 'til you see it!!

I looked at the tired clothes hanging in my closet and sigh. The money I made working part-time after school at The Voltage, a popular coffee shop downtown, had to go toward helping Mom with the bills.

I stare at Trinity's words, her excitement contagious. I want some of that enthusiasm. To be a freespirited sixteen-year-old, just for one night.

I'm supposed to work at nine

I'd have to lie. I hated lying. I suck at it, my eyes always give me away.

Say you're sick. C'mon, Izzy, you've got to go!!

The door of the bathroom I share with my sister opens. Steam billows around Renée's body as she sashays out in a bath towel.

"You plan on showering before school? You'd better hurry up," she says, crossing the chilly cement floor to her bedroom on the other end of the basement. "I can smell the deep fryer on your skin from here." The door closes and she's gone on a whiff of the lavender body wash she adores.

I lift my arm to my nose and inhale. Yep, French fries. Lovely.

I gotta go. See you at school, k?

I roll out of bed and dig around in my drawer for clean underwear, my best pair of holey jeans, and the t-shirt Renée gave me for my birthday. She said she'd chosen the grass-green shade because it matched my eyes. Then proceeded to ruin the moment by adding the sweetheart neckline would give my flat chest a boost. Mom gave her hell over it, but I didn't care. The shirt was the nicest thing in my wardrobe.

"You girls have five minutes and then I'm coming down there," Mom threatens.

She said the same thing every morning. One of

these days I'm going to wait her out just to see if she follows through. Probably not anytime soon, though. The curse of the middle child; trying to keep everyone happy.

The shower goes from tepid to frigid just as I lather up the bird's nest on top of my head. My hair is the bane of my existence. Renée's sleek blond curtain does just what she asks of it. With his sandy hair and freckles, Benjamin gets a break for sheer cuteness. And then there's me. My hair color is a cross between a penny—not the shiny, pretty ones, the old, tarnished kind—and a copper kettle. The curls came from the postman; at least that's what Dad always used to say. Three years of living without my dad have subdued the pain. The heavy weight in my chest gives lie to the claim.

I swipe the mirror with my hand and stare at my reflection. The girl looking back at me seems so much younger than the person living inside her body.

"Izzy, the bus is here. You want to walk to school?" Mom's voice is louder, as though she'd dared a few steps into my sanctuary.

"I'll be right there," I call, anxious to have her leave.

"Well, hurry up then. I have things to do," Mom snaps.

I turned away from the flare of anger in my eyes and methodically dress. My powder blue lacy new bra and panties I'd bought with part of my cheque, the birthday shirt, my jeans—a little snug around the hips —and a pair of flats so I wouldn't raise too much suspicion with my mom.

Because the decision is made—I'm going to the party.

AFTERWORD

Reviews are the lifeblood of any successful author. Without you, we can't be heard. If you enjoy the story, please consider sharing it on your favorite social media sites:

Please click here to post a review:

Amazon

BookBub

Goodreads

Thank you,

Jacquie Biggar

MY GIFT TO YOU!

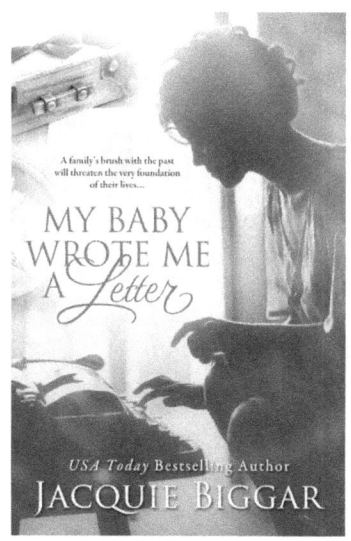

My Baby Wrote Me A Letter

A family's brush with the past will threaten the fabric of their lives.

Eight months pregnant and her Navy husband away on a mission, Grace Freeman craves the security of her childhood home in Canada.

When a letter written by her long-lost mother is found in an old writing desk it creates a tear in the fabric of her family.

Can Grace find a way to bring peace to those she loves, or will a message from the past destroy their future?

Newsletter subscribers also get bonus content and insider information every month. I love giveaways and there is lots of interesting stuff for me to share with you!

Newsletter- Sign up Now!

ALSO BY JACQUIE BIGGAR

WOUNDED HEARTS SERIES

Tidal Falls

The Rebel's Redemption

Twilight's Encore

The Sheriff Meets His Match

Summer Lovin'

Wounded Hearts Box Set

Maggie's Revenge

With This Heart

The SEAL's Temptation

Secrets, Lies & Alibis

MENDED SOULS SERIES

The Guardian

The Beast Within

Virtually Gone

GAMBLING HEARTS

Hold 'Em

Crazy Little Thing Called Love

My Girl

Married to The Texan- Box set

BLUE HAVEN

Sweetheart Cove

Sunset Beach

MEN OF WARHAWKS

Skating on Thin Ice

The Player

THE DEFIANT SISTERS DUET

Letting Go

Finding Me

SINGLE TITLES

Silver Bells

The Lady Said No

My Baby Wrote Me A Letter

Tempted by Mr. Wrong

Valentine: A Hearts and Kisses Romance

Mistletoe Inn

The Sister Pact

Perfectly Imperfect

Love, Me

ABOUT THE AUTHOR

Jacquie Biggar is a USA Today bestselling author of romance who loves to write about tough, alpha males and strong, contemporary women willing to show their men that true power comes from love. She lives on Vancouver Island with her husband and loves to hear from readers all over the world!

In her own words:

"My name is Jacquie Biggar. When I'm not acting like a total klutz I am a wife, mother of one, grandmother, and a butler to my calico cat.

My guilty pleasures are reality tv shows like Amazing Race and The Voice. I can be found every Monday night in my armchair plastered to the television laughing at Blake's shenanigans.

I love to hang at the beach with DH (darling hubby) taking pictures or reading romance novels (what else?).

I have a slight Tim Hortons obsession, enjoy gardening, everything pink and talking to my friends."

Subscribe to her Newsletter and follow her on these sites:

Amazon | Website | Facebook | Newsletter
Twitter | Pinterest | GoodReads | Bookbub